Only With You
(The Connor Family, Book 4)

LAYLA HAGEN

Dear Reader,

If you want to receive news about my upcoming books and sales, you can sign up for my newsletter HERE: http://laylahagen.com/mailing-list-sign-up/

Chapter One
Carter

"Carter, you're doing it wrong. You're supposed to make bows, not knots," my five-year-old niece informed me.

Peyton sat on the dining table, dangling her feet, giving me a severe look while I worked the ties at the end of her dress sleeve.

"Guys, come on. I don't want to be late on the first day. It's a new school. I need to make a good impression," April called from the hallway.

"I'm going to ask April to do it," Peyton said impatiently.

"Okay. Off you go."

I kissed the top of her head before helping her down. She skittered toward her older sister. I looked at my two ladies, smiling even as April rolled her eyes at me. She was almost fifteen. Eye rolling came with the territory. Peyton usually thought I walked on water, except when I couldn't pull off the style she wanted… which happened all the time.

Once they were both ready, we headed to the

underground parking lot of the building.

"What's with the smug smile?" I asked April as we drove off.

"I love this car. People will notice it. They'll think I have a cool uncle."

I was driving the black Porsche this morning. I owned two other cars. What could I say? I had a weakness for automobiles.

"April, I am cool." I attempted to sound serious.

"Umm... being on Forbes's list of top whatever means you're rich and successful, not cool. Plus, none of my friends read Forbes. Now, if you appeared on TMZ or Hollywood Reporter...."

For three years in a row, Forbes had included my law firm in their top recommendations in the Los Angeles area. Business was booming, which was why we were moving into a larger office this week.

I was getting the keys to the place later today. It was a week of changes for all of us.

"TMZ and Hollywood Reporter don't care about lawyers."

"Well, no, but you could date an actress. Or a model. Someone cool. You're definitely great-looking. Moms check you out all the time. I don't get why you're single. Being single sucks."

"Language, April."

I glanced at Peyton in the back seat. She was humming a song to herself, oblivious to our conversation.

I hid my smile, focusing on the road. I liked

keeping the girls in the dark about how active my dating life was.

But then I replayed her sentence in my mind, zeroing in on a particular detail. Being single sucks, she'd said. How would she know? She hadn't brought boys home yet. April was a great kid, but I sensed that my laid-back, anything-goes parenting style wasn't going to work as well in her teenage years as it had for the past five years.

"You have a boyfriend?" I asked casually, trying to sound more like the cool uncle and not the overbearing uncle. April was a beautiful girl. Both girls resembled my late sister tremendously, April especially. She'd inherited Hannah's dark brown hair and eyes. Peyton had her mother's hair but her dad's eyes.

"Considering it," April said nonchalantly. "I can't wait to invite new friends over to our apartment. They'll be psyched. Everyone loves our flashy place."

"Girlfriends?"

April narrowed her eyes, pointing a finger at my chest as if she wanted to stab me with it. "Oh, no! You do not get to police me. I can have any kind of friends."

"Yes, of course, you can have any friends you want. But I would like to know who you bring over. If you're bringing boys, we will need some rules."

She raised a brow. "Really? And you think I'll listen because you're a fancy lawyer?"

"April, you know I don't like policing you.

But I'm the adult here, and even though you're old enough to make decisions, I'm responsible for you. Rules aren't to encroach on your territory but to keep you safe. We'll have to compromise on things."

That was a very lawyerly way of saying that I was in charge. There were things on which I wanted to put my foot down. Did she want to wear a short dress at school? No. Piercings and tattoos? No and no. Staying out after ten o'clock? Negotiable. Inviting over a boy when I was not at home? Hell, no. But I had to find a smart way to lay out my rules. I was one of the top lawyers in the Los Angeles area. Opposing counsel had been known to drop cases when they'd found out they were going to face me. But I didn't want to raise the girls like a despot.

April sighed. "Carter, you're becoming less cool by the minute. Just thought you should know."

I was sure Hannah was looking at us from somewhere above and having a good laugh. Before she and my brother-in-law passed away, I'd done nothing but stomp on all the rules, always taking April's side. Whenever I was visiting, I'd take her shopping, buying everything her parents wouldn't. It had been five years, but I still missed my sister every day.

After I pulled the car into the parking lot in front of the school, I half turned, grinning at the girls.

"Ready to go?" I asked.

April grinned back, and Peyton squealed from the back seat. It was a big day for my girls. I planned to take them out for a treat tonight, to spoil them a bit.

An hour later, I held in my hand the keys to the new offices of Sloane & Partners. The building manager, Kate, had given me a tour of the space, and as we neared the end, she said, "I'm hosting a charity event for deaf and hard of hearing children. Would you like to participate? It's in one month."

"Email me all the details. I'll send a check if I already have something planned."

"Sure. But I'd love to have you there. I manage a few buildings in the area, and all my clients are participating. Even the owner of my big fish, as I like to say, Valentina's Laboratories. It's the huge gray building around the corner. Big name in cosmetics and fragrances."

The name didn't ring a bell, but since I wasn't involved in that industry, it wasn't saying much.

"She invited some of her Hollywood connections, so the place will be packed with celebrities. Might be good for business," Kate rattled on.

"As I said, send me all details."

"Will do. Okay. That's it from me. If you need anything, give me a call. When are your movers bringing the furniture?"

"Later today. We'll open up for business tomorrow."

"My, that's quick, but I suppose you don't build a reputation like yours by being anything other than sharp."

"It's necessary. Our clients don't like to wait."

"I'll leave you to do your thing, then. Welcome to your new office. I might be biased, but I think you'll like it much better here."

Chapter Two
Val

I called my sister Hailey as I flagged down a cab, grateful that this terrible date was over.

"Hey, sis! Where are you?" I asked when she picked up. I knew she was out with our other sister, Lori.

"Uh-oh. Date over so early?"

"Yep. Are you two still out? I can join you."

"Right." Hailey rattled off the address just as a cab pulled in front of me. They weren't far away, which was a relief. Traffic in LA could be madness. I tried to push my crappy date to the back of my mind as the cabbie sped through town.

Half an hour later, I walked inside one of the many beach bars along Santa Monica, twisting my waist-long dark hair into a bun at the base of my head.

My sisters were sitting at a high bar table in one corner of the terrace. Hailey waved enthusiastically. As I approached them, I noticed three glasses of cocktails.

"What's this?" I pointed to the third glass.

"You sounded like you needed it," Hailey explained.

"So we thought we'd be prepared," Lori added.

I climbed on the chair, sipping the cocktail. Yum; it was delicious.

"Spill it," Hailey said. "The secret to getting over a bad date is to describe it in extraneous detail so we can commiserate with you."

"Chad seemed like a nice guy," I began. "You know, on paper. Decent job, not too bad to look at. He had no sense of humor, but hey, you can't have it all, right?"

"Yes, you can," Lori said with a dreamy smile. She was married to a great man.

"What happened?" Hailey asked.

"Turns out he's an ass. Was checking out the waitress right in front of me."

Hailey wrinkled her nose. "Ugh. You do have bad luck, sister."

For the past two months I'd been seeing this guy, Ethan. Two weeks ago I discovered I wasn't the only woman he was seeing. The humiliation of finding out still stung. One of the reasons I'd gone out with Chad tonight was to move on from that. The joke was on me.

"What if it's more than bad luck? I think I must give off the wrong signal."

I was usually a confident and optimistic person, but my recent experiences had done a number on me.

"Valentina Connor," Hailey said carefully, "you are one of the smartest and kindest women I know, and you have great fashion sense. Don't doubt yourself."

She pointed to my attire—a dark green summer dress that reached my knees and brought out the green in my eyes. I'd paired it with black flats. I was tall enough even without heels. Hailey almost always wore sky-high heels.

I drank some more. "You have to say that, though. We're related. You can't be mean to me."

Lori chuckled. "No, but we wouldn't lie."

Well, that was true. My family rarely minced words. I could count on them to be honest. I looked at them warmly, happy I could spend the end of this evening with them. Others needed ice cream after a bad date; I needed Hailey and Lori. They weren't just my sisters, they were my best friends. We were a team, whether we were on a shopping spree or relentlessly teasing my brothers during our weekly Friday dinners. Yeah, we had the kind of family dynamic that often made people wonder if we were grown-ups after all, but it worked for us.

"Val, what's wrong?" Lori asked, pushing a hand through her blonde hair. "You're usually optimistic. Is it the issue with Beauty SkinEssence?"

My stomach rolled. The second reason I'd accepted a date with Chad was because I'd been desperate to take my mind off that.

I nodded. "I have a meeting with a mediator tomorrow."

"Val, you have nothing to worry about." Hailey put a comforting hand on my shoulder.

LAYLA HAGEN

I owned a cosmetic and fragrance company, Valentina's Laboratories. My team had developed a formula for an antiaging cream, and now one of the multinational conglomerates were claiming they'd done it first. There was no patent, and they hadn't advertised it anywhere. The only mention had been in a French trade magazine three months ago, but we'd been working on our formula for nine months at that point. I was fairly certain that what Beauty SkinEssence wanted was for me to drop the line, because if we launched similar products at the same time, profits would shrink for both sides.

The company was my baby. It had taken me twelve years to grow it to the successful business it was today. I wasn't going to allow anyone to threaten what I'd built or smear the hard work of my team by calling us copycats. I looked up from my cocktail to find my sisters exchanging a glance. I suppressed a smile, certain that I knew what would follow.

"So, it looks like we have to plan an intervention," Hailey told Lori, confirming my suspicions.

I laughed, throwing my head back. God, I seriously loved these girls. Interventions were a common thing in the Connor household. Whenever we thought one of us needed some shaking up, we'd pull one. If shit hit the fan, an ambush was needed.

I had introduced the concept of interventions at twenty-one. After our parents died in a car crash, my twin brother Landon and I took care of our sisters and two brothers. In that difficult time, we needed the goofing and silliness that came with interventions. But the tradition stuck to this day. At thirty-six, I loved it as much as I had in my early twenties.

"How about I make you a deal? You wait until after my meeting with the mediator. Otherwise you might have to work on another intervention tomorrow."

"We don't mind," Lori assured me. Hailey backed her up with a vigorous nod.

"Nah, we don't have time. I should get going. I need to be up early tomorrow. The meeting is at eight o'clock."

I'd insisted the mediator come to me so we could have that first conversation on my territory.

Despite leaving after only having one other drink, it was close to midnight when I arrived home. Alone in my house, I started fretting over the meeting again. My company wasn't just a way of making money for me. It was who I was.

I put together my outfit for the next day, as usual. Doing so bought me time in the morning, when I would sell pieces of my soul for a few extra minutes of sleep. I'd taken out a fire-red pencil skirt and a black blouse with a sleeve that hung off one shoulder. It wasn't exactly typical office attire, but I loved it, and it was weather-appropriate for mid-September. As a plus, it was my lucky outfit, and I was determined to turn around my luck.

Chapter Three
Val

Next morning, dressed in my lucky outfit, I stopped by Walter's, the coffee shop across the street from my office building. It was the closest one, and I liked to start the morning by buying a cup of coffee before heading to work.

I usually ran into a few patrons I knew, people who worked at some of the other offices nearby. I waved to the head of the HR department of a beverage company with whom I'd had lunch a few times.

Then I slid my gaze over the perimeter for anyone else I might know. My gaze fell on the stranger in line next to me, and I straightened a little, paying extra attention. He was taller than me (and the lucky outfit required me to wear heels). His shirt stretched over a broad chest and a tapered waist. His strong hands ended in long fingers that made me wonder if he played the piano. I even got a fleeting look at his face as he turned to study the menu. His hair was almost black, and I was sure that his eyes were hazel, providing a beautiful contrast.

I hadn't realized I was staring until he unhitched his gaze from the board displaying the menu and turned to look at me. He was absolutely gorgeous. I'd been wrong; his eyes weren't simply hazel. They had golden flecks too. I broke the eye contact as my turn came. I ordered my usual— cappuccino with whipped cream and caramel topping.

While waiting for my drink, I discovered that I'd developed a wandering eye that was intent on surveying the stranger, cataloging every detail. He joined me in the waiting corner. Now he was close enough that I couldn't look at him without being obvious. But oh, I could smell him. I recognized the cologne instantly. It wasn't one of mine, but it was a favorite nonetheless. I concentrated on the sweets display, my mouth almost watering at the sight of the blueberry pancakes. Nope. I'll be strong today. No pancakes.

Our drinks were placed on the counter at the same time. The stranger reached for his first, but the server must have placed it too close to the edge, because it toppled right over… knocking mine as well. I jumped backward as the hot contents spilled everywhere.

"I'm sorry," the stranger said. Ah, that voice. Just another tool in his arsenal to make him more irresistible to poor souls like me. "I'll buy you another one."

"No need."

"I insist. I knocked it over."

A man with manners. Will you look at that?

"Well, if you insist, I won't say no."

We went back to the cashier.

"A cappuccino with whipped cream and caramel topping for the lady. And a blueberry pancake," he said.

I looked at him questioningly. "Why did you order that?"

He gave me a half smile and a wink. "Saw you looking at them earlier."

I smiled, caught by surprise. I hadn't felt like smiling all morning. I'd woken up in a frenzy, with my heart in my throat. I'd hoped that sticking to my usual morning routine would keep the nerves about the potential lawsuit at bay. But until this beautiful stranger had made me laugh, my insides had been twisted together like a vine.

"Well, you caught me there. And since you bought it for me, I can't let it go to waste, can I?"

The stranger gave me a crooked smile. He motioned with his head to one of the empty tables. "Shall we?"

I glanced at the time on my smartphone. "I only have twenty minutes."

"Plenty of time to drink our coffees and for you to enjoy your pancake. By the way you were looking at it, it wouldn't last longer than five minutes anyway."

Had he just called me out on my appetite? Yes, yes, he had. But since he was spot-on, I couldn't argue with him. Walter's was cozy, with its vintage tables and chairs and comfortable couches. We sat at a table by the window. When he'd draped the jacket of his navy suit over the backrest of the chair, I'd had a prime view of his ass. Well, hell. Now that was a detail I wanted to remember.

"Do you work at one of the companies in the area? Or are you here for a meeting?" I asked.

"I just moved my company here. You?"

"My office is nearby." I didn't feel like giving him any details, because any mention of my company would bring the upcoming meeting front and center again. "I stop here every morning for coffee."

He set an elbow on the table, leaning slightly over. "And a pancake?"

"Occasionally."

"Come on, you can be honest with me." He winked, and I couldn't help laughing. How could he tell that by occasionally I'd meant every other day?

"Well, I might indulge more than just occasionally. Might."

"I see. Too early in the morning for honest confessions?" He was teasing me, and I enjoyed it immensely.

"Way too early," I confirmed, and now he was laughing. We chitchatted about nothing in particular while we drank our coffees. He wasn't offering any details about himself. We hadn't even exchanged names.

I wondered if, like me, he didn't want to think about the day ahead. Usually people liked to brag about their jobs, and judging by his expensive suit and watch, he had a brag-worthy job. I liked the anonymity of our conversation. It was freeing. This enigmatic stranger was hands down the best thing that could have happened to me this morning.

When it was time for me to leave, he stood up from his chair at the same time I did. I really liked his manners. Our arms touched as we both moved. The contact only lasted a second, but my entire body reacted. What was wrong with me? Was I so starved for affection that the slightest touch affected me so much? Okay, so it was the touch of a tall and gorgeous man, but still.

"Do you have any recommendations for lunch places?"

"Mrs. Seguin." I answered with the first name that popped into my mind, because I planned to head there for lunch. "It's great for business meetings too. They have a wide selection."

"Thanks."

"I need to hurry," I said regretfully. Without realizing it, I'd motioned with my head across the street to my building.

"You work at Valentina's Laboratories?"

"Yes. I'm the owner, Valentina. You know the company?" The name was written next to the entrance door, but the font wasn't large enough to be seen from across the street.

"We have the same building manager. She told me about you."

Kate was a darling. She bragged about me to everyone.

"I'm Carter."

Ah, a sexy name to go with a sexy man.

"I'd love to stay and chat some more, but I have to prepare for my meeting."

"Have a nice day, Valentina."

The morning took a nasty turn when my lawyer called me frantically to inform me he'd been in a minor car accident on the freeway and couldn't make it in time for the meeting.

"We should reschedule," he said at once.

"The mediator will arrive in a few minutes. I'll deal with it."

After all the hassle it took for both parties to agree on the law firm we'd use for mediation, I wanted to get this over with as soon as possible.

I spent the next ten minutes behind my desk, surveying the notes I'd made during my conversation with my lawyer. As I reviewed the notes, I committed everything to memory. I wasn't going to take them into the meeting. I felt more confident when I spoke freely, and I was determined to appear strong and unfazed, not as if I would bend to the competition's demands.

At five to eight, my assistant knocked on the open door. "He's here, Val. I already led him to the meeting room."

My palms instantly felt clammy, but I sounded calm as I spoke. "Okay. Offer him water, or coffee or—"

"Poison?" Anne suggested cheerfully.

"If you do, you cannot involve me. You're on

your own." I grinned. "Just tell him I'll be there in a few minutes."

I rose from my chair as Anne disappeared from view, then strode with large, confident steps. I wouldn't allow anyone to take me down, or smear my name, not after working for this dream for more than a decade.

The meeting room was just a few feet away from my own office, and when I stepped inside, the mediator introduced himself as Emerson Smith.

"My lawyer can't make it this morning," I told him after inviting him to sit opposite me.

"Would you like to reschedule?"

"No, there is no need. Let's get on with it. What are their demands?"

"Ms. Connor, I will lay everything out in simple terms. They don't desire a lawsuit any more than you do. All they ask of you is not to bring that line to market."

I bristled, moving at the edge of my chair. "All they ask? That would mean admitting I was wrong."

I crossed my arms over my chest, staring at the wooden table between us. "They have no patent or credible base from which to point their finger at me. We developed the same product at the same time. A hundred copycats will catch up to us two months later anyway. It's not patentable."

"They will sue if you insist on bringing it to market. You know this is about profits, and nothing else. By the time the copycats will bring out their product, they could make a nice profit. But if you bring it out at the same time, it will cut into their profits."

"I cannot tell my team to trash their work. As I said, agreeing to their terms would be akin to recognizing I was in the wrong." I licked my lips, searching for a way to make him understand it wasn't just about the money. "This... I know for them this is just a small branch. A profitable one, but just a blip on their portfolio of products. For me, it's everything. I built this company."

"I understand your viewpoint perfectly. How would you solve this? What would you like me to tell them?"

"Tell them that I don't see any reason we can't both bring our products on the market. Sure, it will mean lower profits for both, but that's business. You win some, you lose some."

Emerson went on to share a few more details, but the meeting was surprisingly short, and I was frustrated that nothing at all had been resolved. I'd been hoping to put the issue behind me, but I'd clearly been too optimistic.

This wasn't my first rodeo with a bigger player on the market trying to intimidate me. Since I'd listed the first line in Sephora, the sharks had started showing their teeth. Once I was big enough to be noticed, they tried to push me out. I got it, store placement was limited already, and the perfume and cosmetics industry was cutthroat, with thousands of fragrances being released every year from big houses alone. So far, none of those intimidation attempts had resulted in actual lawsuits. I was betting on this going the same way.

The rest of the morning was busy as hell. I had an open-door policy, which meant anyone could stop by anytime with a question or a problem. My stomach began rumbling around ten o'clock, but I did pull through until twelve when I practically ran toward Mrs. Seguin.

The place was already half full when I arrived, but I found a table and was lazily perusing the menu, even though I already knew what I wanted to order. I was just about to flag down a waiter when I saw a certain tall and spectacularly handsome someone step inside the restaurant. Carter.

He saw me immediately and began to walk my way, smiling. I smiled back. I had a feeling my day was just about to become better.

Chapter Four
Val

"Valentina, we meet again."

"Call me Val. Everyone does."

"Are you waiting for someone?"

I shook my head.

"Can I buy you lunch, then?"

I laughed. "We can eat together, but you don't have to buy my lunch."

"I insist." He'd said the same thing this morning. I narrowed my eyes.

"You are very insistent, aren't you?"

He didn't bother denying it. I sat a little straighter in my chair.

"Well, I insist too. You're not buying lunch."

He watched me with amused but determined eyes. I cocked a brow, enjoying our silent standoff. Eventually, he realized I wasn't going to back down and relented with a nod before drawing back his chair and sitting down.

"What's good here?"

"The fries, the guacamole, the crab. Honestly, everything is delicious. I usually order the special of the day."

"I'm going to trust you."

LAYLA HAGEN

A waiter stopped by, and we both ordered the special and sparkling water.

"How was your morning?" Carter asked once we were alone.

I grimaced. "I don't want to think about it at all. Tell me about yours. How come you decided to move to this area?"

"My law firm outgrew our old offices, and this area is getting a lot of attention."

My shoulders slumped. He was a lawyer? I felt extremely deflated that my sexy stranger wasn't so far removed from my troubles as I'd thought. Was he a ruthless lawyer? Possibly heartless? What kind of cases did he take? Was he the type who would represent a large multinational trying to crush a smaller player to enhance their profits?

I inwardly chastised myself. After the morning I'd had, I wasn't feeling very friendly toward lawyers. But that wasn't fair to Carter, so I tilted my lips in a polite smile.

"It's becoming very popular. I moved my business here years ago when it wasn't nearly as lively. I love it. Has a sense of community."

"Speaking of community, Kate invited me to the charity event. I've looked it up. That's a great cause."

"It is. Are you coming?"

"Yes. I cleared my calendar."

I smiled. A heartless man wouldn't look up the details of a charity, right? Right?

24

***

Carter

Our order arrived, and we dug into our food in silence. I used the opportunity to observe Val as I'd done at the coffee shop. She'd caught my attention when she stood in line in front of me, and I had had an excellent vantage point. She was stunning and funny as hell. The fifteen minutes I'd spent with Valentina this morning had been the highlight of my week.

When I entered the restaurant just now, I noticed her hair first—those long, thick tresses cascading down her back. I could only imagine what it would feel like to sink my hands into it, tugging while I pulled her closer.

Even now, I couldn't look away from her. She was beautiful, with that black top hanging off one shoulder. I was taller than her, so this morning I'd had an excellent view of her cleavage when we stood in line. My mouth watered just remembering.

Midway through our lunch, my phone vibrated with an incoming message.

"Sorry, I just have to check if it's something urgent."

April: I'm going to a movie with some people from my English class. I'll be home late.

I groaned, then remembered I wasn't alone. Val was watching me curiously.

"Trouble at work?"

"No… it's my niece," I admitted reluctantly.

"She's just texted me to say she'll be home late. She informed me, didn't ask me. This will set a bad precedent. She's fourteen."

I had no idea why I was telling her this.

Val rested her elbows on the table, watching me intently. "Let me guess... you want to be firm with her, but you also don't want her to hate you?"

"Yes. Exactly. How do you know?"

She gave me a small smile. No, wait a second. It wasn't a small smile. More like she was fighting the urge to laugh. "Want some advice?"

"Yes, please."

I already had my parents' advice on this, but I wanted a third party's opinion. Since the girls had come to live with me, Mom split her time between LA and Montana. My father still owned the fir tree farm he'd had while I was growing up. After Hannah's death, Mom wanted to be closer to her grandkids. She'd just retired from her job as a teacher and had taken up freelance editing, so she was flexible. I'd rented an apartment for her and offered to move them both permanently here, assuring them I could cover their financial needs, but my dad was too proud for that. The farm was his life, even though he was bound to take things slower now. He was about to have hip surgery. Mom had flown to Montana the week before the girls started school, and this time she was staying there for a few months.

"You need to be firm. She'll hate you for a bit, but then she'll get over it. It's important to make her understand that you don't want to control her. Also important—choose your battles."

"Makes sense in theory. Now I just have to find the right way to formulate it."

This time she did laugh. And since this morning I'd laughed with her, I could tell the distinction—now she was laughing at me.

"You're a lawyer. I'm sure you know how to get your opinion across," she pointed out.

"Different skill set, I'm afraid."

"I see."

"Do you?"

I usually didn't talk about my nieces. People didn't care, but Val seemed interested. I liked that a lot.

A waiter passed by, asking if we wanted the tab. I nodded, even though I wanted to drag out our lunch date because I hadn't had nearly enough time with her, but I had a meeting across town.

I automatically reached for the tab as the waiter brought it, but Val put her hand on a corner.

"No, mister. We're sharing the tab. We agreed."

"I didn't explicitly agree."

Her jaw dropped, and her green eyes were so full of fervor that I wanted to kiss her until she wrapped those long legs around me and begged for more.

"That's not how I remember it. You nodded."

I held both hands up in surrender. "True, true. I'm a man of my word."

"Uh-uh. I'm not sure I believe you."

She glanced at me suspiciously right up until we each paid, then said, "Before I forget, have you confirmed with Kate that you're coming to the event?"

"I haven't gotten to that yet, but I'll send her an email."

"I have access to the guest list since I know some of the guests. I'll put you on it. It's going to be great, even though it's going to be tiring for me. I'll have to mingle a lot."

But mingling didn't last the entire night. After everyone had a few cocktails on board, it was pointless anyway. They wouldn't remember the conversation the next day. The venue where the gala was taking place was surrounded by a large garden. I could take Val out for a stroll after she was done mingling, maybe share a glass of wine in private, get to know her better. Get a taste of those lush lips too.

I'd been fantasizing about tasting them since this morning. I'd barely kept my thoughts in line, which was a definite first. I'd always been able to keep a clear head at work. But I kept reverting to that view of her cleavage. If I sucked on a nipple, would she roll her hips against me? How responsive would she be to my touch?

She took her overlarge phone out of her bag, setting it on the table.

"Let's see, here is the guest list." She pulled up a spreadsheet. It had four columns. Name, Plus one, Email, Phone Number.

My imagination had been spiraling out, but it

came to a screeching halt when I saw there was a name in the Plus One column next to Val's name. She was going to the event with someone. Was it just a date, or did she have a boyfriend?

I was fighting to clear my thoughts as Val asked, "Are you bringing a plus one?"

"No."

"Can I have your last name, email, and phone number?"

"Sloane." I rattled off the other information, trying to digest my disappointment.

"All done."

I rose first from my chair, then held out hers. She glanced up in surprise.

"I take manners seriously."

"Clearly."

"Thank you for keeping me company, Val."

I couldn't help myself and leaned in closer than was polite when she rose. The little sigh of surprise she let out was delicious.

Chapter Five
Val

Friday dinners were a religion in the Connor family. I liked to call it regrouping time. No matter how shitty or exhausting a week, these few hours I spent surrounded by my siblings filled me with energy. I liked knowing what everyone was up to.

While I was cooking, Ethan called. I'd deleted him from my contacts list, and when I saw a random number calling, I answered thinking it could be related to the charity event.

"Hey, Val."

I straightened as if someone had electrocuted me. "Ethan. Why are you calling?"

"Listen, I know we've had our differences—"

"You were cheating," I said through gritted teeth, leaning against the counter.

"We never said we were exclusive."

I blinked repeatedly as my insides twisted. It was true, he'd never specifically said we would be exclusive, but I'd always thought it was implied anyway. How could I have been so gullible? God, I was a moron... always dreaming, always hoping. Being cheated on stung like hell.

"What do you want?"

"Let's start again with a clean slate."

"Not interested."

"Don't be like that. We could talk about it. Tell you what. We can go out for dinner before the charity event."

"You're not coming to that."

True, he'd been my plus one, but he thought he was still invited?

"Val, come on. You promised you'd introduce me to that producer."

That was why he'd called? Because he was still hoping for that introduction? I felt so small. So small. I wasn't going to allow anyone to make me feel that way.

"Ethan, in case it's not clear, this is me revoking that invitation. Don't call me again."

I punched the End Call button, breathing in through my nose. I felt lost, but I had to pull myself together. My siblings would arrive for dinner in no time. They'd sniff me out instantly if I kept the long face, and I didn't want our dinner to turn into moping hour.

Landon and I spoke briefly about my beef with Beauty SkinEssence when he arrived. I had no update, since I hadn't heard from them since the mediation meeting three days ago. My twin had set up the company with me before moving on to do his own thing and becoming a wildly successful businessman.

When Hailey arrived, I worked on my poker face. To no avail.

It took her exactly seven minutes to point a finger at me and say, "Wait a second. Why do you look like you need an entire bottle of Pinot Noir for yourself? You aren't laughing with your eyes."

"What?" I asked.

"When you laugh, or smile, your eyes seem a little sad."

Shit, well, the cat was out of the bag. There was no point denying it. I gave in and told her about the phone call with Ethan.

"God damn that idiot," Hailey hissed. "You know what, I'm going to give him a piece of my mind."

"No, you will not. He's not worth your time."

"Yes, but how else will he learn his lesson?"

"Let's change the subject, or the boys will sniff us out."

Hailey and I were bringing in the food while my brothers were setting the table, together with their better halves. Well, except for Jace. My soccer star brother was the odd one out, still single. My twin, Landon, was happily married to Maddie, the genius who had designed the garden outside my house as well as the one at the office. They also had a daughter, Willow. Will was engaged to Paige.

Lori and her husband and son were the only ones missing tonight. Pity, because I'd been looking forward to hugging my nephew, Milo.

Lori had been a single mother for seven years before she fell in love with Graham, and I was used to her and Milo being at my house a whole lot more.

I missed spending time with that little boy.

Hailey grinned. "That wouldn't be so bad. There would be no holding them back."

I popped open a bottle of Pinot too, for good measure. The sour alcohol matched my soured mood and heart perfectly. Belatedly, I also realized it sent a clear signal. Our wine system wasn't a secret: Pinot for moping, Chardonnay for celebrating.

Jace materialized right next to us.

"What's with the Pinot?" When Hailey didn't answer, he trained his eyes on me.

"Nothing serious."

"If it's serious enough for Pinot, then it's something I should know about."

My mind was working at top speed, looking between Jace and Hailey. I knew that if I insisted on keeping things to myself, Jace would lure it all out of Hailey, who'd never learned to keep family secrets. Hmm... the best course of action was definitely to break the news myself. That way I could leave out a few details so my brothers wouldn't flex their alpha muscles.

"I ended things with the guy I was seeing. Ethan."

"What did he do?" Jace asked at once.

"Turned out he was seeing other people too," Hailey informed him. "And now he called to ask if he could still go with her to the charity event so he could schmooze with some producer."

I groaned. So much for keeping the details to myself.

"What?" Hailey asked defensively.

Jace narrowed his eyes. "Where does the guy live?"

I'd thought there was any way to keep them from being overprotective? I was dead wrong.

"On the moon, Jace. Just forget about him. I intend to."

But Jace kept his eyes narrowed. "I can find out even if you don't tell me." He glanced briefly at Hailey, but I wasn't worried. Hailey didn't know where Ethan lived.

But then Jace motioned to Will, who joined us in an instant.

"That Ethan guy screwed our sister over. She won't tell us where he lives." Jace certainly didn't mince words. Will's gaze turned murderous. Shoot. Now I was worried.

"I can find out where he lives," Will assured him. He used to be a detective. I was sure he still had enough connections to the police to find out anything. I was losing the battle. Truthfully, I didn't even know how to fight in these situations. Plus, a tiny part of me did hope my brothers would accidentally run into Ethan. They didn't even know what he looked like, because I'd never introduced him to the family, but a girl could dream.

Was I a terrible person or what?

Jace turned to me, asking in a soft voice, "Sis, are you okay?"

I nodded with conviction. "We hadn't dated for that long."

"Yes, but I know you. You put so much of yourself into everything."

"I think I'm slowly learning my lesson." My brother's concern warmed me. Even though I gave them shit, I was beyond happy and grateful that my family rallied around me no matter if I dealt with a lawsuit or a bad date.

And I really couldn't point fingers.

I was always poking my nose in their business and offering my help whether it was required or not. I was slowly trying to rein in my instincts, but who was I kidding? They were part of who I was.

Those instincts partly formed after my parents passed away and Landon and I had been forced to take charge. But this nosiness had always been ingrained in my personality. My nature had cost me some relationships too, with boyfriends telling me I was too meddling.

"You need a date for the charity event? I can come," Will offered.

Jace grinned. "I'm offering myself as potential companion too, sister. You can have your pick."

"I don't need an escort. I can go by myself."

It was a pity Hailey couldn't come—she worked at a PR agency in Hollywood, and she was the one who'd put me in contact with the celebrities I'd invited.

I suddenly remembered Carter would be there, and my mood improved drastically. I'd taken an instant liking to him when he'd spoken about his niece. He was obviously close to his family too. I usually tended to see the best in everyone, but I didn't think I was so far off base with Carter.

Of course, those piercing hazel eyes and overall delicious package might cloud my judgment.

I smiled as we all sat at the table, ready to dig in. My ranch-style home always felt too big, except during Friday dinners.

When I'd bought the land and built the house on it, I might have been overly optimistic about my love life. It was that optimism that had gotten my heart into trouble so many times.

I wasn't giving up on love, but I did plan on taking things easier. Much easier.

Chapter Six
Carter

"Come on, man. It's Friday night," Anthony said. "Stay for one more round of drinks."

"Yeah, the next round is on me," Zachary added.

They were my partners at Sloane & Partners. We'd taken out our entire team of twelve for drinks, to celebrate the move to the new office.

"Have fun. I need to get home to the girls."

There were several boos from the team, but I shook my head, smiling.

"You should bring them too," someone said.

"At a bar?"

"We can move to a restaurant."

"I promised I'd watch a movie with them."

"Awww... that's so sweet." That was Ashley, one of our interns.

Zachary shuddered. "Ashley! Don't say that in public. Imagine if word went out that the great Carter Sloane's employees call him sweet? His reputation would be ruined. Our entire business would collapse."

Clients flocked to us because we had a great track record. They trusted my ability and work ethic, and appreciated my no-nonsense attitude.

"Hey, who knows? It could be a unique selling proposition. Most people think lawyers are soulless robots," Ashley volleyed back.

"Could be true," I said.

"Nah, boss. You're not fooling anyone," Ashley said.

I liked to think I was the kind of boss everyone liked. I was ruthless when I had to be, but I liked the casual atmosphere. The law business was exhausting as it was. We could all do without the additional pressure of a stressful office life.

As I waved goodbye to everyone, I caught Zachary eyeing Ashley suggestively. I cocked a brow, motioning him to follow me. Once we were far enough from the group, I went straight to business.

"No fucking around at the office."

Zachary set his jaw. "I know the rules."

"You weren't looking at Ashley as if you were planning to follow the rules. Employees are off-limits." My tone was harsh, but I wanted to get my point across. Even though we'd been friends since law school, rules were rules.

"Understood."

"Good. Have fun."

He didn't look too happy with me as I left, but there was nothing I could do about that. Office hookups weren't unusual in bigger firms. I understood the appeal. The hours were long and the pressure was always high. It was a way of relieving tension. But in a smaller firm like this one, it was too risky, too messy.

The truth was, the number of singles or divorcees in the industry was alarming. The long hours were not exactly family- or relationship-friendly. And Zachary didn't have anything to complain about. He hooked up often and wasn't even discreet about it.

I dated plenty, but I hadn't had a real relationship in some time. I wasn't averse to them, but after the girls moved in with me, things changed. Some women pulled back when they found out I was a package deal or drifted away after I introduced them to the girls. After trying and failing a few times, I stopped trying. It was the best for the girls, and for me.

The girls and I ended up watching movies late into the night and sleeping most of Saturday. On Sunday I treated us all to ice cream and asked them about their week, trying to gauge if they liked the new school and were settling in well. As always, the weekend went by too fast.

On Monday morning, I headed out earlier than usual because I wanted to stop by the coffee shop first. That coffee was damn good, and so were the sandwiches. And who knew? I might even run into Valentina. She's taken, I reminded myself, but then another voice at the back of my mind assuaged my guilt. We could just enjoy each other's company or be friends.

Yeah... except every time I thought about

her, the images flashing in my mind weren't of the friendly variety. I wanted to taste her. Not just her lips. All of her.

I swept my gaze once around the coffee shop when I entered and found Val at one of the corner tables. After receiving my order, I went straight to her. She didn't see me until I was right in front of her.

"I see you're on your way to becoming a fan of Walter's," she said.

"It's a nice place to start off your morning."

"I know, right?"

"Mind if I keep you company?" I pointed to the chair next to her.

"Please."

Being this close to her made it impossible to keep my thoughts in line. I didn't just want to kiss her, I wanted to wrap my hand in her thick, luscious hair, draw the tip of my nose up and down her neck, then follow the same trail with my mouth.

"You have something in your hair. I think it's a... plastic flower?" Val asked, amused.

"What?" I ran my hand through my hair. Sure enough, a tiny flower was stuck in it. Very masculine.

"Looks like this came off Peyton's dress when I hugged her this morning." Hugging was a mild term. She had climbed in my arms and refused to let go until I promised to take them out for ice cream tonight. I caved, of course.

"Your fourteen-year-old niece?"

"No, that's April. Peyton is the five-year-old."

At her questioning glance, I added, "They live with me. My sister and her husband passed away a few years ago, and I'm their guardian."

"Oh. I'm sorry for your loss." Something flickered in those beautiful green eyes as she added, "They keep you on your toes, huh?"

"You can say that. My parents help as much as they can, but they live in Montana. They have a fir tree farm there."

"How did you end up being a lawyer in LA?"

"I studied at UCLA for my undergraduate degree, and I liked the city. And as to why I became a lawyer, let's say that I've always been argumentative. Could talk my way out of everything."

"Oh, I can imagine."

As a guy who worked outdoors a lot, my dad made fun of me for doing the exact opposite and then going daily to the gym.

"Now you have to smell other people's sweat to make up for being on your ass all day," he'd chortle gleefully. I laughed every time. It was true, even though training helped me clear my mind. The rush of endorphins improved my focus. I liked my career, and it was very lucrative. I could make sure that Peyton and April attended the best schools and wouldn't have to work odd jobs to put themselves through college as I had.

"How did you end up building a cosmetics and fragrance company from the ground up? Your story is fascinating."

"You looked me up." Her mouth popped

open, as if she couldn't imagine why I would do such a thing.

"I did."

"Well, there's a lot more to it than what's on the website."

"Tell me all about it."

"Sorry, I can't right now. I'm pressed for time and really have to get going. I have a million things to do."

"Are you looking forward to the charity?"

"Oh, yes."

"Is your date also in the cosmetics industry? Or film?"

She cast her eyes downward to her cup of coffee. "He is in the film industry. But I'll be going alone."

"Your date got caught up at work?"

"No, we're just not dating anymore."

I shouldn't rejoice at her obvious disappointment, but I couldn't help the fist-pump feeling that overtook me. I wanted to get to know this woman better.

"What happened?"

She shrugged as if it didn't matter, but I could tell that it did matter to her. I didn't push the issue, though. It clearly made her uncomfortable, and why should she share something so personal with me, after all? We barely knew each other. I set out to take her mind off it instead, all the while trying to ignore the thought that she wasn't taken anymore.

"No pancake this morning?" I asked.

"Nope."

I leaned in a little closer, touching her forearm, craving the contact. Her gaze dropped to my hand on her arm, and she licked her lips.

"How about if I buy it for you? Does that count?"

"It definitely does."

"But your conscience wouldn't be guilty."

"You're even better at finding tricks and loopholes than I am." She smiled at me.

"What if I buy two for me and then decide I've had enough after the first one? Would be a shame to let the other go to waste."

"You never run out of arguments, do you?"

"Not when I'm after something," I admitted.

"And what you're after now is me having a pancake?"

It crossed my mind to lay out my cards and tell her exactly what I was after, but I couldn't be that direct. Yet.

"I want to turn this morning around for you. Don't let that moron waste more of your time than he already has."

I kept her gaze for a beat, then another one. I could tell she didn't want to look away first, but eventually she did, shaking her head and chuckling.

"Do you always employ such dangerous tactics to lift someone's mood?"

"I'd categorize this as ballsy, but I'm happy to show you my dangerous side too."

Val swallowed. "Well, I'd love to find out

exactly how you distinguish ballsy from dangerous. I have a hunch that our definitions differ, but duty calls. I must do some things for the charity event too. At this rate, it's feeling more like work than fun."

"We'll enjoy ourselves too."

"Define enjoy," she challenged with a smile while pulling her hair into a ponytail. The movement of her hands made her chest rise and push forward. She bared her neck. That skin looked so kissable, so touchable that I was barely fighting the urge to find an excuse—any excuse—to touch her. I looked at her mouth long enough for her to notice. Her eyes widened. She felt the chemistry between us too.

"Nah, and spoil all the anticipation? I'll show you when we're there."

I rose from my chair at the same time as her.

"I've been to enough events to know they're not my kind of fun."

"But you didn't have me to keep you company."

Her lips parted slightly. Then she narrowed her eyes.

"Well, then… I could use some fun. I look forward to seeing you in action. I'll hold you to it."

"I'll make sure you do."

Chapter Seven
Val

I was a little light-headed as I sat behind my desk. The first thing I did when I opened my laptop was to look up Carter online. I felt giddy, as if I was doing something I wasn't supposed to. His law firm was three-years-young, but that was still impressive, considering he was thirty-five. The lawyers I knew who'd set up their own practices had done so later in their career.

I googled him a bit, and it was apparent he was a very successful litigation lawyer.

I was dying to know more about him, but I reluctantly went back to the to-do list I'd written yesterday evening, cross-checking it with some of the more urgent emails in my inbox. I usually didn't have trouble concentrating in the morning, but I caught my thoughts wandering more than once and had to make a conscious effort to whip them back into line. When the screen of my phone lit up with an incoming message, I reached for it, even though I avoided answering messages during the day. Too distracting.

Carter: Are you free for lunch?

I'd given him my phone number during our

first lunch, right before we parted ways.

Val: Nope. We have some deadlines coming up, and I'm eating in my office.

Carter: Any restaurant recommendations?

I smiled as I typed the names of a few restaurants.

I tried to push him out of my thoughts for the rest of the day, but it proved to be a challenge. That sinful smile and those hypnotizing eyes kept popping up in my mind.

In the afternoon, he texted again.

Carter: Want to grab a coffee?

Val: Do you ever work?

Carter: ;-) in between breaks.

Carter: Can I tempt you with a coffee?

My heart rate picked up. I tried to ignore it.

Val: No can do. Plus, you can't keep hijacking my working time. I have a no-messaging policy, and usually only check my phone during short breaks (which I spend here).

Carter: When exactly do you take your breaks?

Val: At 11a.m. and 4p.m.

It was now 3:09 p.m. I hadn't thought Carter would stop texting, but I hadn't expected his reply either.

Carter: Perfect. I look forward to hijacking your time during your breaks.

I laughed. And now I had even more trouble focusing, counting down the minutes to four o'clock, wondering if he'd start his hijacking campaign today or tomorrow.

Shaking my head, I concentrated on the email I was composing. I wanted to run three focus groups for the upcoming Goddess campaign for one of our fragrance lines. We'd already had one, but I hadn't overseen it. It turned out to be the wrong thing to delegate. The moderator hadn't explored all facets, hadn't asked all the right questions. I could do better, and I wanted to. It wasn't easy to run focus groups for fragrances. They were luxuries—an aspiration, but since they didn't serve a specific purpose the way antiaging creams did, it was hard to build a unique selling proposition. It was why the majority of the industry was banking on sexy and sensual ads to sell them. But fragrances meant something more to me than making me feel sexy. They were memories in a bottle, and dreams too, and somehow I could only convey that to focus groups if I was there in person.

After firing off the instructions to my marketing director, I discovered an email from Hailey. My sister respected my no-messaging policy... but only because she'd found the email loophole.

I smirked. Hailey was much like Carter in this regard.

Subject: URGENT

Discovered that the brother of a coworker is a CATCH. Maybe even has potential to be "the one." Want me to introduce you to him?

I sighed, shaking my head. This was urgent? I could punish Hailey with silence, but knowing my sister, she'd get overexcited and set things in motion without waiting for my reply.

Val: Nope. Hold your horses.

The one. She was spitting one of my favorite phrases back at me. Sometimes I felt foolish for using the expression. Over the years, I'd dated a lot and had had a few relationships. Some had been longer, some just for fun—especially right after Jace and Hailey moved away from home. But I had a tendency to romanticize relationships. I couldn't deny it. It was one of my faults.

I shook my head as I reread her email. I was determined to stick to my newfound resolution of taking it easy.

I turned off the computer screen, jotting notes on paper instead.

Carefree, childhood-favorite memories.

Same for vacation. Ask for exact details (especially of places) and infer associated fragrance notes.

Asking for direct smells rarely worked because people couldn't identify individual notes. To anyone looking from outside, my notes wouldn't make much sense, but this process worked for me. I started with keywords and half phrases and eventually developed questions.

I had almost forgotten about Carter, but at four o'clock on the dot, my phone buzzed. I startled in my seat. Each and every thought about the focus group flew away.

Carter: Tell me something about you.

I blinked at the screen. Even though I didn't

understand the purpose of the question, I drummed my fingers on the back of the phone in excitement before texting back.

Val: Like what?

Carter: Whatever you want. Something that's not obvious.

Val: I like to sing when I'm alone.

Only after I'd sent it did I wonder if it was a strange thing to admit.

Carter: Do you also sing in the shower?

Right. I wasn't going to answer that.

Val: Your turn.

Carter: What gave you that idea?

Val: A question for a question?

Carter: Nah, I ask all the questions.

I toed off my shoes and tucked my legs under me in the enormous leather chair.

Val: But what's in it for me?

Carter: Your breaks will be much more enjoyable.

I laughed, taking a few seconds to collect my thoughts.

Val: Don't assume they weren't enjoyable before. You know what they say about those who assume. An answer for an answer. My first and last offer.

His reply didn't come right away, but when it did, heat oozed right between my thighs.

Carter: If it pleases you.

The little dots indicating that he was composing a message appeared, and I waited with bated breath for the next words.

Carter: In that case, we'll need more than ten minutes per break.

I leaned my head back, smiling at the ceiling. Was he negotiating? Well, he was in for a surprise, because this was one of my strongest areas.

Val: No can do. Ten minutes is all I can give you.

He didn't write anything back, and I glanced at the clock on the display. 4:11 p.m. Damn. He was going to leave me hanging? Two minutes later, after I still had no reply, I shook my head and went back to my to-do list, even though I sneaked a glance at my phone now and again.

Over the next two weeks, Carter messaged me at 11:00 a.m. and 4:00 p.m. on the dot. I'd gotten my way, pushing my own questions when he tried to cheat (which he did every time). I even asked his professional opinion on my beef with Beauty SkinEssence. His response had left me scratching my head. As a lawyer, he advised me to avoid a lawsuit. On a personal note, he said he'd fight for what he thought was right too.

Even so, I looked forward to his messages more than I wanted to admit. I told myself that this was just a fun way to pass the breaks. We were two adults caught up in whirlwind careers and needed to let steam off. Some people gambled or did worse to that end. By comparison, exchanging fun, flirty messages seemed innocent. But when I ran into him at the coffee shop one morning, I couldn't ignore the current of awareness passing through me when Carter greeted me in that deep voice of his. It wasn't innocent at all.

"Morning."

"Hey!"

"I was hoping I'd find you here."

"Is that so? Why?"

We stood in line next to each other, and I couldn't help leaning in just a bit closer. He smelled amazing. He was an amazing package all around, truth be told. Carter was a classically handsome man, with striking eyes and lips and a body that belonged on the cover of a magazine. Next thing I knew, our cheeks were almost touching. He'd leaned in too.

"What time do you start work? And when do you finish?" he asked.

"Eight to six." I had no idea why he'd asked that, but then the corners of his lips tilted up in a knowing smile.

"Why?"

"Told you I need more than ten minutes. Since you're not relenting about your break times, I found an alternative."

Being only inches away from him was making a mockery of my negotiation skills. The man was too compelling.

"You're assuming again."

"Am I?" He'd leaned in even closer, and I barely bit down the urge to touch that freshly shaved jaw. I nodded, but I was grateful that my turn came next. I ordered quickly, asking the cashier to pack everything to go.

"It's still seven thirty, Val," Carter whispered in my ear. "You have time to eat breakfast with me."

"I have to look over some notes for a meeting."

He didn't push at all, which was surprising.

What I'd told him was true, but it wasn't the only reason I wasn't staying. Maybe I should stop the flirty messages. He had just moved his office across the road from mine. If this flirting went south, things could become awkward.

In truth, I was having too much fun to stop.

So when Carter texted me at eleven on the dot, I texted right back.

Chapter Eight
Val

"Oh, these are so beautiful."

I was shopping for an outfit for the charity event, and in true Valentina Connor fashion, I had too many favorites to decide. I twirled around, admiring the light blue dress from all angles. I placed three more dresses into the maybe pile. I was just about to ask the sales associate to bring me some shoes as well when my phone pinged. Carter. After the encounter at the coffee shop yesterday, my heart went pitter-patter each time I saw his name.

Carter: Thanks for the advice regarding April. Finally talked to her, and she agreed to (some of) my terms and hasn't forsaken me as an uncle.

Val: Yet. Don't underestimate her.

Carter: Let me savor the victory a while longer.

Val: Wouldn't want you to get too comfortable.

Oh, Carter. He was a captivating man, that was for sure. And of all things, it was his voice I couldn't get out of my mind. Whenever he spoke in that rich voice of his, I felt it like a physical caress in my intimate parts. Just remembering it had the same effect. It made me feel weak that I couldn't ignore this magnetic pull toward him.

I inspected the blue dress again. Attending such events required dressing up for show, and it was a good excuse to treat myself to a gorgeous designer dress. My phone kept distracting me. I had a new message.

Carter: Ready for tomorrow?

My stomach flipped.

Val: I'm shopping for it right now. Buying an outfit. Dress to impress.

Carter: I'll wait for you at the entrance. I'm going to be the one in a tux ;)

I grinned. Every man there would be wearing a tux. I tried on every dress, deciding on one that was bright yellow, with a thin belt made of black velvet around my waist. The dress barely brushed my knees and had wide straps over my shoulders. The bodice was more of a corset, pushing my breasts together. Sexy, but not over the top. Just what I needed. I glanced at the price tag and tried not to feel so guilty. It was about 20 percent more expensive than what I'd intended to spend, but what the hell? I worked hard. I deserved to treat myself to this beauty. I waged this inner battle whenever I was splurging. I supposed the guilty feelings were baggage I carried from the time when we were pinching pennies, after we took over Dad's pub.

I snapped a picture of myself in the yellow dress, sending it to Hailey. We usually shopped together, because sharing the experience and commenting on each other's outfits was half the fun, but she couldn't swing it this time.

Carter: I'm impressed.

GOD. NO. WHY?

How had I mixed up the senders? My face heated up. The pose was a little silly and a lot sexy. The dress had a slit on one side, which wasn't visible unless I showed off one leg. And show off I did. I was also pushing up a boob with one hand and winking in an exaggerated manner. It was the kind of picture I'd never send to anyone but my sisters.

Val: That was meant for my sister. So she could vote on her favorite.

Carter: Haven't seen the other options, but... HELL, YES!

Well, that was embarrassing. I debated typing a reply, then decided I'd pretend this hadn't happened.

Next evening, my palms were sweating a little as I climbed out of the cab in front of the venue where the reception was taking place. I was comfortable with a large range of people, from salesmen to scientists. The latter were my favorite, since I'd majored in chemistry. But thanks to Hailey, a good-sized group of stars had shown up, and the Hollywood crowd was another story altogether. Which was why, I told myself, I was relieved when I noticed Carter at the bottom of the staircase leading up to the main entrance of the villa. My stomach flipped like it was trying to win a gold medal at the

Olympics. He was waiting for me, as he'd promised, and wearing a tux.

His eyes crinkled at the corners when he smiled at me. I didn't know where to look first. Those hypnotizing dark eyes or the delicious way he filled out the tux.

"Just as gorgeous as I remember." He surveyed me from head to foot before we climbed the staircase. "Yellow becomes you."

I blushed. Well, there was the flaw in my plan. I couldn't pretend the picture incident hadn't happened unless he played along.

"Can we forget about the picture?"

The corners of his mouth twitched. Oh, boy. He wasn't going to let this go.

"Only if you promise to show me the others too."

It took me a second to realize he meant the pictures of the other dresses I'd tried on.

"Absolutely not," I said heatedly as we stepped inside.

"Why? Were they even sexier? Tell me." He leaned his head in, as if beckoning me to whisper in his ear. I pushed him firmly away by the shoulder, then pointed my forefinger at him.

"I didn't intend to send it to you."

He tilted his head, smiling even wider. "Well, the effect it had on me was lasting even if it was… unintended."

I had no reply for that, so I just pretended to inspect our surroundings. My head was turned in the opposite direction when I felt Carter inch closer.

"You're the most beautiful woman here tonight, Valentina."

I waved a hand dismissively. I didn't fall for such lines anymore, especially after my last dating fiasco reminded me that LA was the city where the most beautiful women gathered to try their luck in acting, singing, or modeling. But when I turned to look straight at Carter, something in his expression told me it wasn't a line.

Or maybe I was just too naive.

One of the organizers noticed me and motioned that she needed to talk to me. Carter saw her too.

"I'll go see what she needs," I told him. "Then I'm going to do the rounds. I have a list of about twenty people I need to talk to."

"Go ahead. We'll have plenty of time to talk later."

The event was every bit what I had expected. Three hours into it, I was almost used to the constant chatter as background noise. I'd already spoken to quite a few of the celebrities I'd wanted to approach for a campaign I was putting together for the spring releases.

After a particularly productive conversation with a young, rising pop star I wanted to feature in our spring campaign, I looked around for a bench or a chair. If I could just sit for five minutes, I was sure the balls of my feet wouldn't feel raw anymore. I had no problems walking in heels, even though I didn't have Hailey's stamina. But standing rooted to one spot was problematic.

I didn't see any empty chairs, and just when I was about to head to one of the smaller rooms to check if the couches there were full, a mountain of a man cornered me.

"Hey, you," he said.

"Hi, Gus!"

We'd spoken earlier in the evening. He was one of the models I was courting for a marketing campaign. He'd gained in popularity over the last year, and he could be going places. I wanted to snatch him before he became too expensive.

"Want to grab a drink?" he asked.

"Thanks, but I have yet to finish my rounds."

"Oh, come on. Don't be a spoilsport."

He seemed to have already had a few drinks. His footing wasn't too certain. He was looking at me as if I was something to eat, and I didn't appreciate it. I usually got out of this type of sticky situation by flashing what Hailey liked to call my scary face, but this one wasn't budging.

"Not being a spoilsport, but duty is still calling."

The guy cocked an eyebrow, and instead of backing off, came even closer. Oh, hell, no. I didn't want to cause a scene, but if this guy didn't take a hint, I'd have no choice.

It was then that a movement behind the guy's shoulder caught my attention. Carter was standing a few feet away, looking at us. When I caught his eye, he mouthed, is he bothering you? I nodded imperceptibly, and Carter strode right to us. I thought he'd simply say he needed to talk to me, but before he even opened his mouth, he curled an arm around my waist. He pulled me so close that the side of my breast was squished against his chest.

"There you are. Thought I'd lost you." He stuck out his other hand to Gus. "Carter Sloane."

Gus shook it reluctantly. Carter pressed me even closer. My nose was almost touching his jaw. The smooth skin on his cheek and the faint smell of aftershave indicated that he'd shaved just before coming here.

Gus looked between us, then left without another word. Even so, Carter didn't let go. My body buzzed along the contact points—the length of his arm against my back, the side of my boob against his chest—as if the contact was skin on skin. The way he was holding my waist was almost possessive. And I loved it.

"Are you okay?" he asked.

"Yes. I was just debating how to get rid of him before you showed up. Lucky you saw me."

"I haven't been able to keep my eyes off you all evening." As if just now realizing there was no reason to hold me anymore, he let go. I wished he hadn't.

"Still need to make the rounds?" he asked.

"Yeah. Still have to talk to a few people. Are you enjoying yourself?"

"Already made some contacts. It's a great event." He kept his gaze firmly on my face. In fact, so firmly that it made me wonder if he was making an extra effort not to look down. Or maybe that was just wishful thinking on my part. "Find you later?"

I nodded, and after we parted ways, I mingled again. I breezed through the remaining people on my list. Two of the conversations were a waste of time, two were semiproductive.

I was looking forward to the fun part of the evening. What exactly did Carter have in mind?

Once I was done, I headed to the bar, ready for my first alcoholic drink this evening. A glass of Chardonnay would do me good. I'd only had some water until now, wanting to keep my mind focused.

The bar had been set up in one of the rooms that opened up directly onto the back terrace. It was crowded, and I wedged myself between two guys, waiting my turn. The back of the bar was mirrored, and I watched the movement in the room. My body was starting to relax now that I'd already spoken to everyone I needed to.

But then I noticed a familiar face in the crowd, and every inch of my body went on alert again. Carter was heading toward me. Our gazes met in the mirror.

He stopped right behind me and whispered in my ear, "Ready to get out of here?"

Our gazes were still locked in the mirror. He'd brought a hand to my lower back, resting it there, as if the fact that he'd touched me once had broken some barrier between us.

"I have to be here at the end for the raffle." Everyone had bid on donated items ranging from art to around-the-world trips, and the winners would be announced at the end.

He was now feathering his hand up and down my back. I kept my composure as long as he was touching my dress, but when I felt three roughened fingers on my bare shoulder blades, I couldn't help the sizzle that went through me.

"You don't trust me to bring you back by the end of the evening?" His voice was playful and conspiratorial, but his eyes had a deliciously dark and edgy glint.

I swallowed, licking my lips. Somewhere in the past seconds, he'd moved so close that my arm was pressed along his chest. At least it wasn't my boob this time. People were crushing in on us from all sides. Was he so close because he wanted to be or because he didn't have another choice?

"We'll just disappear for a few hours, take a much-needed breath."

"You promised we'll enjoy ourselves, remember? Taking a breath sounds... boring."

His expression changed to a smile that was downright... wolfish. "I didn't say that will be the only thing we'll be doing. So? Trust me?"

I nodded, finally turning around so I wasn't looking in the mirror, but at him directly.

"What do you want to drink?"

"Chardonnay."

"A bottle of chardonnay and two glasses, please," Carter ordered.

"We don't need an entire bottle," I whispered to him.

"I know, but it's easier than carrying two full glasses."

While we waited, more people crammed in around the counter, squishing us together. Carter was right behind me, and I had to make a concerted effort to keep my ass from pressing against his crotch.

"You smell amazing," he murmured against my skin. When I felt the tip of his nose on the side of my neck, a white-hot sizzle shot through me, making every muscle in my body strum. Oh, God... how could that tiny contact set me on edge like this?

When the bartender finally set the items on the counter, I grabbed the glasses by the stems, while Carter took the ice bucket with the wine bottle. Then he interlaced our free hands and led me through the crowd. He was holding me as if I belonged to him. My pulse thrummed in my ears as we made our way through the packed room, and then the terrace. We descended the marble steps and stepped into the garden. The crowd thinned the more distance we put between ourselves and the building.

"This garden is huge," I commented.

"You've never been here before?"

"No. You?"

"Several times."

We slowed our pace now that we'd escaped the crowd. Carter let go of my hand, pointing to a narrow alley lined with evergreens on both sides.

"This way."

I walked next to him, enjoying the sudden quiet. It seemed a few degrees cooler too. We walked until we came upon an opening on the right side of the hedgerow.

"Wow." We entered a smaller, private garden with a fountain in the middle. It had a circular edge made out of stone that was wide enough to sit.

"Can we sit there?"

"Sure."

"Oh. I've been dying to sit all night."

"After you." He chuckled, keeping a hand on my lower back as we headed toward it. Now that we were alone, the contact felt different. Intimate.

As we sat down he uncorked the bottle and poured wine in each of the glasses, which we then clinked.

"How do you even know about this place?"

"This is open to visitors during the day. I brought April and Peyton here last year, and they gave us a tour of the gardens. And whenever I'm here for an event, I take a walk when I need a break."

Alone? I wanted to ask. Or did he pick up someone at every event? I pushed that thought to the very back of my mind. How could he be so handsome? His dark hair was messy, as if he'd run his hand repeatedly through it tonight. Messy looked good on him, especially because it contrasted so starkly with the tux. He'd taken off the jacket at some point and was only wearing a shirt now. A white shirt that stretched over his abs and chest, showing off his sculpted muscles.

"Where are the girls tonight?"

"Home. They have a nanny who watches them in the afternoon and when I have commitments in the evening. April all but begged me to take her with me. I think rubbing elbows with celebrities earned me a few points in the cool department. Then I lost all of them when I told her she couldn't come. But I've been to enough of these to know it's no place for a fourteen-year-old, especially since I couldn't keep an eye on her."

That was cute.

"Thanks for stepping in earlier when that guy cornered me. Wouldn't have pegged you for a white knight."

"Why not?"

"Just didn't get that vibe." The honest answer was because he was giving off tall, handsome, and dangerous vibes, but I couldn't own up to that. He watched me as if he knew exactly what I was thinking.

Chapter Nine
Carter

I was battling with myself constantly between wanting to talk to this woman, find out more about her, and kiss the hell out of her. She sipped from her glass, making a little sound of pleasure at the back of her throat. I was too consumed by Val to drink. When she raised her gaze and noticed I'd been watching her, she licked her lips, looking away. A whiff of her perfume reached me with the movement of her head.

"Tell me about your perfume. Smells insanely good."

She lit up. "Freesia and lavender. One of Mom's favorite combinations. She gave me the bug for fragrances. We used to make soaps and perfumes when I was little."

This wasn't anywhere on her company's website or in the PR articles I'd come across when I'd looked her up online. She was trusting me with something intimate. There was a wistful expression in her eyes.

"She must be very proud of you."

"I think she would be. They…. We lost my parents more than fifteen years ago." Her voice wobbled for a second, and I squeezed her hand.

I did some mental calculations. Suddenly, I realized why she was so good at giving me advice regarding April. I'd been inexplicably drawn to Val since we'd shared that first coffee, and I wondered if this was part of why. I felt connected to her in a way that took me completely by surprise.

"And you raised your siblings?"

"Yes. Together with my twin brother, Landon."

"You've got four other siblings, right?" I remembered reading that somewhere.

"Correct. And it wasn't easy, but they all grew up into responsible, successful adults. Jace plays soccer for the LA Lords. Will used to be a detective but now runs a foundation with his fiancée. Hailey works at a PR agency. Lori is a wedding planner. I'm so proud of all of them."

"You have every reason to be."

"Thanks."

I liked Valentina's mix of strength and sensuality. And I also loved that delightful side she'd shown in that message she'd sent me by mistake. A picture was worth a thousand words, and that one was going to be my undoing. In fact, it already had been. After we'd exchanged messages, I'd hopped into my shower. All I could think about under the warm spray of the water was how it would feel to take that dress off her, uncover every inch of her sweet body. I ended up jacking off to the fantasy, crying out her name. My dick twitched at the memory.

"Looks like we did need the entire bottle after all," I commented when I refilled our glasses for the third time.

Val giggled. "It was a small one, though."

I wondered why a woman like her was single. When I saw her with that guy tonight, my gut had clenched tightly. They were so close that I'd first thought that they were an item, or about to become one. Then when I'd glimpsed her uncomfortable expression, I saw red. I was proud that I hadn't forcibly removed the guy from her proximity.

"My back hurts from being on my feet for so long."

"Press your thumbs into the quadratus lumborum muscle. It relieves some of the pressure."

"The what?"

Without thinking, I reached to her back, pressing three fingers in the muscle in question. Val straightened, then leaned into my touch.

"Just here."

After I took my hand away, she pressed her thumbs at either side of the spine.

"Ah, that's so good…. Where did you learn about this?"

"From my fitness instructor."

"Figures," she mumbled, more to herself.

"Figures what?"

"That you like to work out." She pointed at my chest, then promptly dropped her hand, as if just realizing what she'd done.

I smiled lazily. "Oh, yeah? You like... the package, Val?"

"I'm trying to decide if my honesty will go to your head."

I laughed, and Val playfully slapped my shoulder.

"Well, you probably own a mirror, and you see what I see, so there's no reason for me to be dishonest."

Despite knowing it wasn't the smartest thing, I leaned closer.

"I want to hear you say it, Valentina."

She narrowed her eyes, as if weighing the pros and cons.

"No, I don't think I will. Too much self-confidence is as bad as no confidence. It's what my dad used to say. He was Irish and tried to pass all sorts of weird sayings as old Irish proverbs, but my friend Google disagrees. I think Dad just made them up. But I like them."

She relaxed—until I moved even closer. "Don't think I'm letting you off the hook about the other thing."

Val licked her lips, then shrugged one shoulder playfully. "Suit yourself. I can't be pressured."

I wiggled my eyebrows. "No, but I bet you can be... persuaded."

"By you?"

"Obviously."

"Mmmm... I don't think so, Mr. Sloane. You

lack the proper persuasion tools."

That was a sweet challenge.

"And what might those be?"

"Think I'm gonna make it easy for you?"

"Give me a hint."

Val spoke the next words with utmost seriousness. "Well, bribery works better than persuasion, if I'm honest. If my sisters are to be believed, I can be talked into crazy things whenever there is ice cream involved. I, on the other hand, can convince them to do crazy things with my famous cheesecake."

Noted.

"I have other persuasion tools."

"Such as?"

I lowered my gaze to her mouth, keeping it there until she darted out the tip of her tongue, wetting her lips.

She flexed her back and wobbled backward a little. I brought a hand to her arm to stabilize her, afraid she'd land in the fountain otherwise. She looked up at me from under those long lashes, and I didn't even register moving my hand from her arm to cup her face, resting my thumb just under her mouth. She parted her lips, releasing a shaky exhale, and I couldn't stay away anymore. I closed the distance between us and spoke against her lips.

"I'm going to kiss you, Valentina."

When she gave me a low moan as an answer, I crushed my mouth to hers. I slid my hand to the back of her head. When I sucked a little on her tongue, she groaned right into my mouth.

With my free hand, I drew her closer. I needed more than her lips. I wanted the warmth of her body, to feel her sweet curves. No, that was a mistake... because now that she was pressed against me, I became greedier still, wanting to feel her skin. I lost all sense of space and time, right until I realized she was whispering my name. Then I pulled her in my lap, moving my hands up her legs.

Her skin broke out in goose bumps. When I moved past her knees, her hips slid forward an inch. When I cupped her ass, my fingers didn't encounter fabric, and for a split second, I thought she wasn't wearing panties. At the thought of her bare, I nearly lost my mind.

I instantly turned rock-hard, and Val felt it because I'd pressed her into me. My hand moved from bare skin onto lace as I ran my finger over the scrap of fabric between her ass cheeks. I wanted a taste of her. I wanted to drop to my knees, remove those tiny panties, spread her wide, and work her with my mouth until she exploded.

I moved my lips down to her jaw, to her earlobe.

"I can't stop kissing you," I confessed. "Or touching you."

"Carter," she whispered, sounding as if she wanted to be kissed again but unsure if it was a good idea.

I held her close to me, resting my nose in the crook of her neck, right up until a loud gong rang from the villa.

"Oh, they're calling us back already." Val sounded as dejected as I felt. I didn't care about the gala, or the prizes. I just wanted more time with her. Something had shifted between us during this hour we'd spent here, and I wanted to solidify that before the night was over.

I took her hand, helping her stand up from the edge of the fountain.

"Always so gallant."

"Never forget my manners."

On the way to the villa, we ran into one of the organizers.

"Val, I'm so sorry I haven't had time to greet you. And you are Ethan, I presume?" she asked.

I clenched my jaw, stretching my hand forward. "Carter Sloane. Pleased to meet you."

"Oh!"

She looked between Val and me, confused.

"Could we quickly go over the prizes you donated before we move inside?" she asked Val.

"Sure."

"I'll be in the villa," I said. Val nodded, not quite meeting my eye.

My gut clenched as I headed inside. I'd forgotten that she was supposed to be here with another man. Did she still have feelings for him? Was she looking for a rebound? I didn't know what this was between us or what it could become, but I sure as hell didn't want to be Valentina's rebound.

I went to return the empty bottle and glasses to the bar, keeping an eye on the entrance. When Val came in, I fell into step with her as everyone headed to the main hall.

She gave me a small smile but still didn't meet my eyes.

I swallowed, trying to gauge what was going through her mind. She was going to announce the winners along with one of the presenters, so I didn't have much time left with her.

Once we were inside the hall, I pulled her to a semisecluded spot.

"Val, if you want, we can forget what happened tonight. It's your choice."

"Mine? What about you?"

"I already made my choice. I don't want to forget. I'd make an effort if you wanted to. But I don't think you do. Judging by the way you opened up to me…. Fuck, I'm getting hard just remembering it."

"Carter," she whispered in a chiding tone, casting her gaze downward.

"You don't have to answer right now. Just enjoy the evening."

We weren't alone again for the rest of the evening, but I kept close. Whenever our gazes crossed, she smiled before looking away quickly. Whenever I put my hand on the small of her back, or on her arm, she leaned into my touch for a few seconds before straightening up and sucking in a breath. Watching her inner battle was delicious.

By the end of the night, I knew I wouldn't rest until Val was mine.

Chapter Ten
Val

On Monday morning, I barely found a place to sit at Walter's. I sat on one of the chairs at a small, round table in one corner of the room, sipping my cappuccino and people-watching. My neck was oddly stiff, because I'd foregone my morning yoga session for some extra sleep, but hey, cheating was good for the soul now and again. I hadn't bought a pancake though. Nature punished too much cheating by bestowing extra pounds.

I was midway through my coffee when I smelled the familiar whiff of mint and ocean. At first I thought I was imagining it, because Carter had been on my mind almost constantly since Saturday. But then his voice reached me too.

That sexy voice that went with the rest of the package, exactly like caramel completed my cappuccino.

"See you found a seat." He was holding a to-go cup.

"Early bird gets the worm," I said on a wink. "Or in this case, the table. It's crazy here on Mondays, so I always come earlier."

He was carrying the jacket of his suit over his

arm, and his shirt stretched over his taut skin and muscles, almost as if daring every woman around to look at him... which they did.

"You're not eating a pancake."

"Nope. Not this morning."

"I see. So Mondays are for denying yourself things you want?" His tone was playful, and I wondered if he included himself in those things.

"It's healthy to exercise self-restraint now and then."

"Might be healthy, but it's no fun."

He looked around for a free chair, but there wasn't one in sight.

"Looks like you're out of luck today," I said. He returned his attention to me, resting his gaze on my shoulders and neck for a beat longer than polite. I lit up everywhere he looked.

"You seem amused by my shit luck."

"Not at all." So why was I teasing him? Erm... well, because he looked teasable, with that impeccable suit and ruffled hair. Also, I didn't know what else to do. I could still feel his lips on mine. Even his taste was fresh in my mind. But my latest dating fiasco was still looming over my head, and I wasn't ready to take the step from flirty messages to anything else.

I was saved from the need to make more conversation by his phone. It rang, and he looked at the screen with a frown.

"Got to take this. Have a nice day."

For a Monday, it turned out to be excellent.

I'd figured out a new perfume formula with my head chemist, which always gave me a sense of satisfaction. I relied a lot on my colleagues, because while I was great at formulas and mixes, I wasn't a "nose," as perfumers were often called. My sense of smell wasn't refined enough for me to make a perfume on my own, though once we decided on the base notes, I loved playing with middle and top notes. I was also happy that I hadn't heard from Beauty SkinEssence. Granted, it had only been a few weeks, but from experience I knew that the more time passed, the higher was the chance of them dropping this.

"You're out already, boss?" Anne asked when I passed her desk late in the afternoon.

"Yep. See you tomorrow."

I was getting real good at this work-life balance thing. I even had time to do the yoga routine I'd skipped in the morning... but I decided to go shopping instead.

As I sipped my coffee the next morning at Walter's, my gaze was glued to my Kindle. I sat at the same table as yesterday, which had three empty seats around it. I was holding my Kindle for everyone to see, which I hoped would send busy vibes to everyone. Soon, I was lost in the pages, and wished I was drinking ice-cold water instead of a hot coffee. Okay, so maybe reading a sexy romance first thing in the morning was not the best idea, because now I was all hot and bothered. But I'd reached a really great part last night and couldn't wait to pick it up again this morning.

"Is this chair free?"

I looked up to my left. Carter was standing next to me, his hand on the backrest of the chair in question.

"Sure."

"I just got a few minutes. My partner, Zachary, and I are meeting a new client this morning."

He motioned to a guy in a suit who was standing in line. I made the mistake of laying my Kindle on the table. The movement caught Carter's eye, and then his gaze locked on the tiny screen. Belatedly I remembered that I used an extra-large font and that I hadn't turned off the device. I rectified my mistake the very next second. Carter was still standing, as if he'd forgotten what he was about to do.

"What are you reading?"

"Just a book."

"I saw the word clitoris. It's what caught my attention."

"Of course it did," I muttered, feeling my cheeks heat up. Ugh. One thing I loved about a Kindle was that no one could know what I was reading. Not that I was ashamed, but I'd never cared for the judgy looks my book covers had gotten. I was a huge fan of sexy guys on covers. The fewer clothes they had on, the better.

Carter finally sat down, looking at me as if this

was the first time he'd seen me. "So, what's the book about?"

"It's a romance. A sexy romance."

His lip curled in a half smile. "I got the sexy part, all right. So this is how you spend your mornings?"

"No, I usually read before going to sleep, but I'd gotten to a good part and couldn't help myself."

"I see. What other genres do you read?"

"You really want to talk about my reading habits?"

"Yes. I like talking to you. I find you to be a fascinating woman. This is an unexpected angle, that's all."

Unexpected angle. Uh-huh. I bet he thought I was some kind of nympho.

"I read almost everything, from thrillers to mysteries. Even the occasional horror. But romance is my favorite. Nothing like some sweetness and sexy times to make me happy. Dreaming about a swoon-worthy hero is a great way to pass the time."

"Raises the bar for real-life dating, doesn't it?"

"Not really. I know it's a fantasy."

Carter set one forearm on the table, watching me with an undecipherable frown. "Do you still have feelings for that Ethan guy?"

I blinked, completely taken by surprise. "Ethan? Not really. We'd only been dating for two months. It's just that... well, I'm still a bit wary. I haven't had the best luck in the dating world, so I'm taking it easy." I shrugged, hoping he'd let it go. Of course he had other intentions.

"I happen to be just as unlucky."

I squinted, because, well... that seemed unlikely.

"You don't believe me?" He sounded amused.

"I can't quite picture it, no."

"Well, that's the honest truth."

He drew his chair nearer to mine, whispering again. "I'm looking for someone smart and with a sense of humor."

We were interrupted just then as Zachary came back, informing Carter they had to go and introducing himself to me.

Carter stood up as I shook hands with Zachary, still looking at me. "Know anyone interested?"

The heat in his gaze had reached lethal levels. He winked as Zachary pulled him away, and I took in a shaky breath.

I sensed that our morning meetings were going to become a thing, and Carter proved me correct the next morning.

When I arrived at the coffee shop, he was already there, sitting at my usual table. There were two coffee cups on the table, and a pancake. When he motioned me to join him, my feet carried me that way almost of their own volition.

"Got here early and got both of our favorites," he informed me.

I sat down next to him. A corner of my Kindle peeked out from my bag.

"Interrupting your reading time again?" he asked with a twinkle in his eye.

"Well, now that you mention it… I was going to read."

I took one bite of the pancake and sipped my cappuccino. Carter's cup was half-full, but he didn't seem interested in it at the moment. His attention was on me.

"Let me guess, yet again you got to a really good part last night, and you couldn't wait to read this morning?"

"Guilty."

"What did the good part say? Please, don't leave out any detail."

I clenched my thighs together. "You want me to… what? Tell you about the characters?"

Carter was even closer now. If he came any closer, he could practically kiss me.

"They are clearly getting more action than we do, so why not hear all about it? Live vicariously through them. I'm all ears. What I glimpsed was pretty hot. Was that all, or does it get hotter?"

Holy shit, I was burning up. Was he for real? How did this conversation already get out of hand?

"You're blushing, so I guess the answer is a hell of a lot steamier."

I cleared my throat. "I'll give you the title. Then you can read it yourself. What do you think about that?"

He considered that for a moment, then flashed me a Cheshire cat grin. Oh, boy. That couldn't be good.

"Only if we can exchange notes and impressions. Critique details, things like that."

We were both laughing now, but there was something of a challenge in his tone. He was baiting me. I wanted to play right into it because this was too much fun.

"I'll be happy to." I was flirting. I knew it. Still, I couldn't stop. It felt good. When I told him the title, he raised his eyebrows so high, they nearly disappeared into his hairline.

"Stumped, are we, Mr. Reader? If you can't handle the title, wait until you read the book."

"Will I regret this?"

"Probably. How are the girls?" I asked, eager to change the subject.

"April's birthday is coming up. I rented a yacht for it. Not sure it was my smartest idea. I can think of a thing or two that can go wrong. But April has just started at a new school, and I know she is nervous about making friends. Parties always help."

"You want to make her happy," I stated.

"Why so surprised?'

"Not surprised, just... I guess I wasn't expecting you to be so sympathetic."

"I moved away from home when I was fourteen to go to high school. I know how difficult it can be. City kids also tend to be mean to those coming in from small towns, bully them. If I can make things easier for her, I will."

I couldn't imagine anyone bullying Carter. His

commanding presence demanded respect, but maybe things hadn't always been that way. In any case, the man was endearing. I sympathized with him. A teenage party wasn't for the faint of heart.

"How many of your friends are going to be there?"

"Zero."

"You're kidding."

"I figured I'll take the opportunity to get to know April's classmates, mingle with them...."

This poor, clueless man. He had no idea what he was getting into. I felt it was my duty to ease him into it.

"Fair warning: they might not want to mingle with you. The word old might also come up. Don't take it personally."

"I'm beginning to think you're right. April already dropped hints that she hopes I won't stick around too much."

I felt completely disarmed because I was fairly certain not many got to see this side of him: a little unsure, a lot out of his depth. As if knowing this was the right moment to strike (he probably did know; he was a great lawyer after all), he said, "Join me."

"Hmm?"

"Come with me."

"To a party full of fifteen-year-olds? Sounds terrifying."

"It will be, which is why I'm hoping you won't be heartless enough to turn me down."

A day out on the ocean? Why should I say no?

Okay, so I could think of one or two reasons but chose to ignore them.

"What would the world say if they knew you're so afraid of a bunch of teenagers?" I teased.

"Probably the same thing they'd say about you if they knew about your reading habits."

The air between us seemed to thicken. We were sitting so close now that I could feel the warmth of his body. I didn't want to pull away, even though his proximity was making me even more hot and bothered than any sexy scene had lately.

Oh, to hell with everything. I wanted fun, to have an adventure. And here was a man who looked like a Greek god offering me exactly that.

"Okay."

"That's a yes?"

"Yes. It's always great to have company when you're chaperoning."

"We won't be chaperoning, Val. The boat has a nice separate deck where we can lie in the sun."

His meaning was clear: we'd be alone. His eyes twinkled.

"Should I bring anything?"

"A bikini and a towel. I've got everything else covered. I'll take excellent care of you, Val."

Chapter Eleven
Carter

On Saturday, I was reminded of April's very first day of school. She was older now, but she still had the same tell-tale signs of nervousness: biting her nails, playing with her hair.

"April, this is your party. You have to enjoy yourself," I told her as we waited for everyone to arrive on the boat.

"And make friends."

"You can't force that. You'll find your own tribe eventually."

Half the party would be comprised of friends from her old school, and half were classmates from the new one.

She rolled her eyes. "You're talking like an adult."

I tried to remember what it was like to be fifteen, when friends were the most important thing in life.

"No, I'm talking like your uncle. You're cool. Don't change who you are just to fit in with new people."

"Aww, stop it," she said good-naturedly. I ruffled her hair. She leaped away.

"Hey, stop. I'm not five years old."

"Wish you were."

"Carter, please be nice to them. Half are already afraid of you."

"Why?"

"They googled you. You have a reputation. And you look intimidating." She poked one arm. "What do you even need all these muscles for? You're a lawyer. You carry out your fights with words. Thank God you won't be around much."

April had been suspiciously excited when I told her about Val. Her friends started filtering in soon after, and I scrutinized them through the eyes of an uncle and a lawyer. No one had tattoos, or piercings, or looked like they were part of a gang. I made a point to look everyone in the eye as I shook their hands. I was checking if their pupils were dilated, which was usually a sign that they took drugs. Everyone passed the test.

I started to relax, which turned out to be a big mistake. Fifteen minutes later, I was in over my head. I'd caught two guys trying to smuggle vodka aboard—I confiscated it. One of them clearly wanted to be more than April's friend. I was about to pounce on the guy when I saw Val on the dock, waving at me.

She was all smiles as I approached. From behind my sunglasses, I took my time drinking her in. She was wearing a knee-length beach dress with a deep neckline. Her bikini was visible too, the bra pushing her breasts up.

"Not going well so far?" she said instead of hello.

"What gave it away?"

"Before you saw me, you looked like you were going to throw that guy overboard."

"He smuggled in alcohol and was leering at my niece."

She grinned. "What were you expecting?"

"You're amused by my shit luck again," I pointed out as I leaned in to kiss her cheek, bringing my hand to her waist too. I didn't just give her a quick peck. I lingered, laying one corner of my lips close to hers. I was going to claim that beautiful mouth of hers today. But I knew I wouldn't be satisfied with a simple kiss. I wanted more from Val, and from the sweet way that she pressed herself into my touch, her sharp intake of air as she returned the kiss on my cheek, I knew she would surrender to me.

I couldn't wait to be alone with her, to kiss her until she was wet for me. I'd work her up until she panted out my name, begging for more.

"Ready for fun?" I murmured in her ear. She smelled fantastic—some flower I couldn't name—but also spicy. The tremor that coursed through her told me everything I needed to know.

"Yes. Is Peyton here too?"

"No, she's at a playdate the whole day. She's not a strong swimmer yet, and being on the boat all day would have been too dangerous for her."

She watched me with warm eyes as we headed aboard together.

April was ecstatic when I introduced her to Val.

"I've heard so much about you, April."

"Really? Well, my uncle kept you a secret until a few days ago."

"Don't worry. I'll keep him out of your way so he doesn't embarrass you."

Wait a second, what?

"You will?" April looked like she might hug Val.

"I happen to be an expert at taming overprotective genes."

My niece was grinning as if this was the best news she'd heard all day. After she went back to her group, which was huddled together at the other end of the deck, I cocked one brow at Val. She blushed and looked away, then peeked at me from the corner of her eye. I stepped closer. She half turned to me.

"So, you're banding with April against me."

"Well, it's best if she thinks someone is on her side."

"You're playing double agent?"

"Not exactly. Let's make ourselves scarce before you ruin the poor girl's party."

"Are you implying that I'm an ogre?"

She tilted her head playfully to one side. "Haven't made up my mind yet."

"I think you just want to be alone with me. To… what was the phrase? Tame me. How exactly do you plan to do that, Valentina?" Her cheeks turned pink, and I went even closer. She licked her lower lip. I almost crushed my mouth to hers. "If I'm going under, I'd at least like to know how."

"Don't you need to get this boat started?"

"Yes, I do. Want a tour before?"

She hesitated.

"No time to tame me during the tour. But don't worry. I'll give you plenty of opportunities later. Come on."

She nodded, even as her eyes flared in surprise.

"This is the main deck, obviously. A little too small for a party of fifteen, but it'll work out." I then showed her the lower level, which was a living and dining room of sorts.

"So we'll be hiding down here for the day?"

"Of course not. The front part is all ours."

There was a smaller deck in front of the captain's cabin that would give us privacy. I'd arranged for two lounge chairs to be brought there, as well as umbrellas, which I'd open up after lowering the anchor.

"I'll be in the captain's cabin until we reach deeper water."

"I'll work on my tan."

That turned out to be a bad idea.

Watching Val take off her dress was like having a private peep show. Her body was even more amazing than I'd imagined. That tall, willowy figure was going to be my death. I didn't know where to look first. That round, perky ass or her sexy-as-hell breasts, which almost spilled out of her top. Her long legs were muscular but in a lean way. I wanted to have those thighs wrapped around me, to suck on her nipples and worship every inch of her.

I'd run my mouth all over that smooth skin, part her legs, and feast on her until she shook with pleasure.

She settled on one of the two lounge chairs. Thank God she wasn't putting on sunscreen, because I didn't think I could watch that and still pay attention to what I was doing. She plugged in earbuds and lay on her back.

Once I'd brought the boat to clear, deep waters, I lowered the anchor and went out to tell the party that we were docking there for the day. We had a few wetsuits, but I didn't think anyone wanted to swim. It was mid-October, and while the weather was sunny, the water wasn't any fun.

Then I went in the front to Val. She was still lying on her back. I sat on the other chair and trailed my fingers up her left thigh. She blinked her eyes open and pushed up on one elbow, tugging out her earbuds.

"What are you listening to?"

"One of Richard Branson's books."

"Which one? My favorite is Business Stripped Bare."

"Oh, I like that one too. This is his newest. I just love his approach to business, and life in general. How he doesn't really take himself seriously, even though he's so successful."

"Exactly. And his advice is down to earth. His

strategies are smart."

"And unconventional."

I was drawn to her on an intellectual level as well. I'd never given more credit to the smart is sexy credo than now. I liked that she was smart, sharp, and still willing to learn despite having achieved so much. I'd met plenty who figured once they'd reached a certain level of success, there wasn't much anyone could teach them.

"Want a drink?" I asked her.

"Yes."

"Anything in particular?"

"Surprise me."

I barely hid my smile as I descended to the lower deck, retrieving the bottle of champagne I'd bought especially for us, as well as ice cream in two cups.

She laughed in delight as I brought it. "Well, you brought out the big guns."

I sat next to her. "You want to tame me. The least I can do is bring out a persuasion tool."

She was laughing even harder now, and it gave me immense pleasure that I'd brought it on, that she was having so much fun with me. I'd only met this woman recently, and yet I looked forward to spending time with her more than I looked forward to anything else. I was determined for her to enjoy herself today. Of course, making her laugh wasn't the only thing on my agenda.

"So, care to share your taming techniques?" I teased.

"I wasn't implying anything… untoward."

Untoward? Who used that word? I couldn't help myself. I moved closer so that when I spoke, my mouth was almost on her shoulder.

"Oh, but I was. Very untoward."

She swallowed but said nothing. I continued.

"I have some ideas. Want to hear them?"

Val cocked her head, looking straight at me.

"You're extra shameless today."

"I saved it all up. Just for you."

She looked away, but I didn't miss her body's response. Her nipples had perked up and were pushing against the fabric of her bra, begging to be freed. I popped open the bottle and poured us a drink. After we clinked glasses, we enjoyed the sun. I'd never seen her so relaxed.

"This day is perfect," she murmured. "Can you show me the captain's cabin?"

"Sure."

I led her toward the cabin, and the moment we were inside, something between us shifted. I was even more aware of her almost naked body than before. Outside in the sun, the bikini was just that, a bikini, but here inside, it was as if she'd stripped to her lingerie just for me. I showed her the most important functions and some cool gadgets.

"I've always wanted a boat," she confessed, placing her hands on the wheel.

"I'm happy to take you out to sea whenever you want."

I was right behind her and had spoken the

words into her hair. Val let out a long breath.

"Really?" she whispered.

"Yes. I like spending time with you."

I trailed my hands on both of her outer thighs, right up to where the fabric ran over her hips. Then I moved my hands further up, to her waist and the sides of her breasts. She let out a small whimper, clasping the wheel tighter.

Everything around us faded. I forgot where we were, and I wasn't even sure I remembered my own name as I swept her hair to one side, kissing her neck. When she gave me a low moan as an answer, I flipped her around and crushed my mouth to hers. I traced my thumb over the knot keeping her bra together. Val stilled completely.

"I'm taking this off," I said. Val didn't answer with words. Instead, she arched her hips. I almost lost control when she pressed her pelvis against my hard-on. "Turn around."

She did as I asked, and the bow came undone after one simple tug. I kissed her bare skin where it was covered before, then opened the clasp lower on her back. The bikini top fell to the floor. The air was so quiet, so full of anticipation. I wanted to feast on her, but I was so greedy for her that I couldn't decide where to start.

I brought my hands to the front, cupping her breasts.

"Oooooh." Her voice shook on the exclamation.

I trailed my fingers down to her navel, then

lower still, right to the edge of the bikini, tracing the line. I was dying to touch her pussy, but all things in due time. I was going to leave that for last. I kissed down her back next, until I reached the bottom of the bikini. It covered too much of her ass cheeks, which was why I moved the fabric on each side a bit, kissing the skin I revealed, then even giving it a small bite.

"Carter, I'm... ohhh."

I flipped her around, and seeing her look down at me with hooded eyes, cheeks pink, was almost enough to make me come in my swim trunks. She stood with her feet apart and I rained kisses on each of her thighs. As I inched closer to the apex, I felt her contract the muscles in her belly in anticipation. I was shaking with the need for her, and my balls tightened when I drew the tip of my nose over the part of the bikini covering her pussy, then pushed the fabric to one side and had my first taste.

Val almost toppled onto me, but I was holding her by her ass. I licked once over her clit, sucking on it, and she tried to stifle a moan. I wanted to eat her out, but I also wanted to watch her beautiful face when she came apart, so I kissed up her belly, taking my time. I brought my hand to her clit, circling it gently, spurring her to tremors.

When I reached Val's mouth, I bit lightly into her lower lip before kissing her.

I worked her up in a frenzy with my fingers. She was holding tight onto my shoulder with one hand. She dipped her other hand in my swim trunks.

LAYLA HAGEN

"Val," I groaned. "Baby. Touch me. Just like that."

She wrapped her palm tightly along my cock, moving her hand rhythmically. How could this feel so impossibly good? I circled her clit faster and moved my mouth to one of her nipples. I twirled my tongue across it, then sucked it into my mouth. She was almost on the edge, ready to tip over. Her breaths were fast and short. I slid two fingers inside her. She was so turned on that all I wanted was to sink in all that wet heat, claim her as mine. When she came, she rode my hand beautifully, my name on her lips, her hand curled around my erection. I wasn't going to last much longer. I was going to—

"Carter, we have an emergency. Are you in the cabin or below?" April's voice came from a distance, but I felt as if someone had thrown a bucket of ice at me. Jesus Christ, what had I been thinking? How could I have forgotten that we weren't alone on this boat? No one could see what was going on in the cabin unless they came inside, but still... I was supposed to set an example.

Val froze. She pulled her head back, eyes wide, then grinned as I bent to pick up her top, helping her put it on.

"I'll be right out," I said loudly. To Val, I whispered, "I'm sorry."

She shook her head. "Go, go. Before she comes and... well, not exactly rocket science to put two and two together."

Chapter Twelve
Val

It took me a few minutes to calm down. I was so on edge that the simple brush of my panties against bare skin was torture. After gathering my wits, I headed to the back of the boat to make myself useful. Someone had tried to swim and gotten a jellyfish burn. Carter had everything under control. The crisis was already over, but I could see another one looming on the horizon. The guy Carter had been eyeing dangerously when I arrived this morning was smiling at April in a flirty way. Carter was glowering at him from the side.

"Come on, let's go back to the front of the boat. The world is full of overprotective brothers or uncles," I mumbled, tugging at Carter's arm.

"And nieces and sisters who think they don't need us," he countered but relented.

When we returned to the front deck, I suddenly became nervous. To give myself something to do, I sat on my chair, took out the sunscreen from my bag, and began rubbing it into my thighs. I always liked to spend twenty minutes in the sun without any protection, to soak in vitamin D, but the sun was too strong now.

Carter sat at the edge of my lounge chair. "I'm sorry about the interruption."

"You don't have to be sorry."

"Val, look at me," he said softly. "Are you regretting what happened in there?"

"No, but I can't believe I completely forgot we were not alone. I'm just ashamed."

"Don't be. It was my fault. I completely forgot about… anyone else on the boat, honestly. I never lose myself this way."

I was now rubbing sunscreen on my arms and shoulders.

"I'll rub it on your back," he offered, but I hesitated. "I'm not going to try anything, Val. Not today. We're not alone. We learned our lesson."

I narrowed my eyes. "Well, I certainly did. But I'm not sure about you."

"Are you doubting me?"

"Yes." Feeling sassy, I added, "I really do."

He laughed, looking at me incredulously. "Try me."

He held out his palm for me to pour cream on it, and after I scrutinized him for a beat, I poured a generous amount, then turned my back to him. He cheated, of course, and didn't simply spread it on my back. Instead, he slipped his fingers under the clasp around my neck, then along the sides of my boobs.

"Think that part will be in the sun?" I teased. My voice was strained, and I was getting more aroused by the second. Especially because having his hands on me made it impossible not to think about how those fingers had felt between my legs. He'd set me on fire with his mouth, but those fingers... they'd been my undoing.

"Can't be too careful." After a few seconds, he confessed, "I can't stop touching you. But that's exactly what got us in trouble before."

I turned to face him, afraid that he'd be too tempted to seduce me otherwise. I was turned on as hell again. I knew it, and by the sharp intake of breath when he looked down at my erect nipples, he knew it too.

"You were right." His voice was a little gruff, as if he was fighting against letting out sexier sounds, like a growl, or a groan.

"About?"

"When I'm around you, I don't seem to remember we're not alone. But I will do my best. Want anything more to drink? I can make you a cocktail."

"Sounds good."

"Any particular requests?"

"Nah, I'll drink anything."

He returned a few minutes later with a Mai Tai. We lay side by side, soaking up the sun.

"Yum... this is delicious. And it's not easy to make."

"I worked as a bartender during college."

"I didn't know that."

"I also had a gig as a fitness instructor. Anything to pay the bills. I had a scholarship, but it only covered a fraction of the costs."

"Wow. Well, this is delicious. It was one of those cocktails I always asked Landon to make." At his questioning glance, I added, "My parents owned a pub. Landon and I ran it after their car crash."

"Must have been hard."

"It was. But you know all about it."

"It's a bit easier for me. When the girls came to live with me, I was older than you were, and already had a successful career, so at least that aspect was stable. And my mother spent half her time in LA."

"Well, Landon and I were running around like crazy, trying to keep the pub and the kids afloat. Sometimes it felt like one little mishap would bring on disaster."

"But you were still dreaming about your fragrance business, weren't you?"

"Yes. How did you know?"

"You said your mom gave you the bug, so I assumed you've had this dream since you were little."

"Well, yes, I did. I used to make notes at night—ideas for fragrances, ways to promote it."

I turned on one side, watching him curiously. I had a direct view of his bicep, and that mouthwatering chest. The cocktail made me feisty. I was imagining myself licking those abs, showing my appreciation for every single muscle. Shit, and I was accusing him of forgetting we're not alone.

"What finally made you start it?"

I whipped my thoughts back into line. "After

Landon and I graduated from a local community college, we sold the pub and got jobs. We were better off financially. I kept working on my business plan on the side, and then one evening, I told Landon I'd like to try, that I'd start small, with a cheap website and production in our garage. He supported me all the way."

"He sounds like a great guy."

"He is. I couldn't have done any of this without him. We worked together at first, and then he went on to start his own business in the software industry. Eventually he sold the company and opened an investment fund. He was in San Jose for a few years, but now he's back."

"That makes you happy."

"Very." I grinned, tilting my head awkwardly to sip from my glass. "Life's always better when your twin is around to tease and annoy."

I wasn't sure why I was telling him all these things. Probably because he was truly listening. With Carter, I could be myself, and I loved it. I'd felt this on that first morning, when I hadn't even known his name. Also, he wasn't judging me, which was a plus. Some of our friends at the time had insisted that I was selfish to even think about opening a business with everything going on.

"Your turn," I said.

"What do you want to know?"

"Confidential information, of course." I'd said it jokingly, but Carter shifted on one side too, training those blazing eyes on me.

"That wouldn't be fair, would it? You haven't shared any secrets."

"Yes, I did," I assured him. "I don't talk this much usually—not with people I'm not related to, anyway. So you can consider everything confidential information."

Still pinning me with his gaze, he inched closer to the edge of his lounge chair. I was at the edge of my own, so our chests were almost touching. Our hips too. I could feel the heat radiating off his body like a physical force.

"I want to know something you haven't shared with anyone, ever," he whispered.

I scooted away, because being that close to him was dangerous. He smelled delicious, and the Mai Tai had been strong. Dangerous combo. Who knew what I might end up telling him?

"You, sir, are very demanding. And you haven't earned the right to know any real classified info yet."

"Oh, but I'll earn it. You know I will." Amusement danced in his eyes. I hadn't moved far enough to be out of his reach, and my tongue stuck to the roof of my mouth as he drummed his fingers on top of my thigh as if it was the most natural thing in the world. It felt as if he was promising me that one day soon we'd finish what we started in the captain's cabin. I didn't need any words. The heat in his eyes and the barely-there restraint in his touch was more than enough.

"Somehow I doubt that," I teased. His eyes

flared, and he pushed himself up on one elbow. His nipple was almost level with my mouth. One lick wouldn't hurt, right? Wow… my thoughts were out of control. I wasn't touching my glass again.

I cleared my throat, attempting to sound serious. "Yep. So, tell me about yourself."

"You're demanding too."

"It's the cocktail's fault, so basically, your fault, since you made it. But to prove I'm not entirely unfair, I've changed my demand from classified information to just… anything about you."

He gave me a charming smile that did nothing to temper my imagination. I was beginning to think it wasn't the cocktail's fault. The man was just irresistible.

He went on to tell me more about his childhood, about his sister Hannah and his nieces. The more he spoke, the more I realized we had a lot in common. I was getting to know the real Carter, but I couldn't help doubting myself. What if I saw everything through rose-colored glasses? I tended to do that, to trust too easily, romanticize everything. I was hanging on to his every word. I'd come here today for a few hours of relaxation and fun (and maybe some flirting), but I was getting more than I'd bargained for.

Late in the afternoon, it was time to bring out April's cake. She'd refused to have any candles, explaining that those were for kids. But apparently no one was too old for a food fight. I instigated it, of course, though in my defense, it was by accident. Sort of. Carter had teased me, and in return I smeared his cheek with frosting. Things escalated quickly. My inner seven-year-old had come out to play.

"I can't believe you've roped me into this," he exclaimed.

"The soul never gets old. We just forget to be children. Another saying of my dad's."

I was surprised at how much fun Carter was having, as if he'd been waiting for an opportunity to unleash his inner kid too. We returned to the shore late in the evening, and I was absolutely not ready for the day to end.

"I'll walk you to your car," Carter offered once we were on land. April's group was a few feet away, waiting for their parents to pick them up.

"No, it's okay. I parked close."

Carter studied me, and as I took the first step back, he said, "Val, have dinner with me."

"Oh!"

"You sound surprised. In case it's not obvious, I'm crazy attracted to you."

I smiled. "Well, that part is obvious." My heart rate picked up, and the frantic beats were making it hard to think straight.

"When are you free next week?"

"No clue, but I'll check my calendar and let you know."

"Monday at breakfast?" he pressed, his gaze hard and determined. I nodded. He inched closer, pushing a strand of hair behind my ear. The brush of his fingers on my earlobe felt intimate. I shuddered with my entire body. Carter didn't miss my reaction, and his lips curled into a seductive smile.

"Have a great evening, Valentina."

Chapter Thirteen
Val

On Monday morning, I woke up so late that I had no choice but to forego both my yoga and the coffee shop. I shot Carter a quick message to let him know I couldn't make it before darting directly into my office. I had to answer a few emails before heading to the sampling room.

My stomach was rumbling, and I needed breakfast. Otherwise I'd end up vetoing all of the samples.

I was just about to ask my assistant to buy me a sandwich and a coffee when someone knocked at my open door. It was one of the girls who worked at Walter's. Marcy sometimes did the deliveries. I'd ordered a few times, which was why Marcy knew her way around the office. She was holding a takeout bag.

"Marcy, what are you doing here?" Had I placed an order and forgotten about it?

"A certain gentleman you've been hanging out with sent these."

"Ohhhhh. Thank you."

I tried not to smile too broadly as Marcy

placed the bag on my desk.

"He'd been sitting at your usual table, then came up to the counter all sexy and cute, asking if we could deliver your favorites."

"Sexy and cute?" I repeated.

"Yep. He's been making everyone's mornings. We don't get too many guys looking like him around here. They all hang out on the other side of the town."

I chuckled, agreeing with her one hundred percent. Carter looked like the stars who graced the Beverly Hills area. I gave her a tip, and the second she left, I opened the bag. My stomach rumbled louder as the smell of freshly made pancakes wafted out of the bag. I took a bite, and then a sip of coffee. It was my favorite indeed.

I shot him a text.

Val: Thanks for breakfast. Great timing.

I didn't know what else to write, so I sent it like that, not expecting an answer. But I received one in a matter of seconds.

Carter: Saw you barreling down the street and directly into your office. Thought you might need reinforcements before you knocked someone over.

The man had great instincts. I'd almost knocked an elderly woman over this morning. My sensory perception wasn't great this early in the day.

Carter: I missed our usual morning chat.

Val: I'm sorry. I overslept and didn't have time.

Carter: Are you sure that's the only reason?

I bit into the pancake, frowning at my phone.

Val: Sure. What else could it be?

Carter: Me.

Then a second message popped up.

Carter: Avoiding me.

Val: Do I have a reason to avoid you?

Carter: You tell me :-)

Val: Nope, not at all.

Truthfully, I had missed breakfast because of him, just not in the way he thought. I'd overslept because I'd fallen asleep very late. I'd tossed and turned, first thinking about him, then dreaming about him. And those were some hot as hell dreams. Our encounter on the boat had served as the catalyst, and my imagination had filled in the rest.

Carter: When do you have time for dinner?

Val: I checked my calendar and it's hectic. I'll be locked up here with my team most evenings. I have time on Wednesday only.

Carter: April has a recital that evening.

Val: Lunch?

Carter: Zachary and I will be with clients at midday every day this week.

Val: Let's push it to next week then.

Carter: It's not what I was hoping for, but okay. Will I see you tomorrow morning?

Val: I'm not sure. We're choosing the final samples this week, so we start at seven. I'm not good company at that ungodly hour, trust me. I'll probably just order in.

I felt a pang of regret as I sent the message. It

was as if the universe was conspiring against us... well, our schedules were, at least.

Carter: You don't have to. I'll take care of that :-) It's another promise.

Well, hell. He certainly knew how to stump me. I had no idea what to reply, so I sent a simple thank you. Then I finished my breakfast, determined to push all thoughts about Carter to the back of my mind, even though all I wanted now was to call my sisters, open a bottle of wine, and tell them everything in detail, dissect every single thing.

I took my notepad and descended to the testing room, determined to focus on the task at hand. The joke was on me. The tiniest connections were enough for my thoughts to fly back to Carter: a whiff of mint, a mention of masculinity.

"Val?" Nicole, the head chemist, asked.

"Sorry, I didn't catch that." I mentally berated myself. I wasn't going to let my team down. We'd all worked hard for this particular line of fragrances. It was launching on three different continents at the same time—an exclusive line for Sephora, one of our biggest accounts.

This line was one of my favorites: a concept of playful scents to remind us of summer all year round. We had our fair share of alluring and seductive lines, but these were meant for the girl hidden in every woman. The little miss princess inside of us.

Sephora had approached me for an exclusive line after I'd entered a similar partnership with a chain of department stores. When I pitched them my idea, they were intrigued, but warned that the sexy angle worked better than playful. I'd made my case about the two not being mutually exclusive, and they'd run with the idea.

The week turned out to be one of the most intense in months. Beauty SkinEssence hadn't contacted my lawyer again. I wished I had closure on the case. No news was good news, but not knowing was weighing on me.

The daily deliveries from Walter's were just the boost I needed to keep on going.

When I received coffee and yet another pancake the second morning, I berated Carter.

Val: You can't feed me pancakes every morning.

Carter: Why not? You like them.

Val: Yes, but variety is good.

Good for my hips, that was. I would've eaten pancakes all day long and twice on a Sunday, but I also wanted to keep in shape. Next morning, I received a yogurt with muesli and honey with my coffee. I dug right into it, savoring every spoonful.

Val: This is yummy. I've never had it before.

Carter: I'm having the same.

I felt as if we were indeed sharing breakfast, even if we weren't in the same spot. Another message popped up.

Carter: This is making my plan to work my way through your deep and dark secrets significantly harder.

Val: Oh, you thought I'd make it easy for you?

His reply came right away.

Carter: No. But no worries, I'm making progress on my own.

Val: What do you mean?

The next message contained a photo. It took me a second to realize it was a screenshot of the Kindle app on his phone. He was reading a book. Oh, God... he was reading my book. The one that had gotten me all hot and bothered right in the middle of the coffee shop last week.

And holy shit, that passage he'd sent me... I'd highlighted it, because it was some of the steamiest stuff I'd ever read. My face was burning, and so was my chest. Hell, I wasn't ashamed to admit (to myself) that I was even burning between my thighs.

What was I supposed to answer? Was he even expecting a reply? I mean... he had to be. Why else send it to me?

Val: So you're enjoying it?

Carter: I can see the appeal. Different from my usual bedtime read.

I bet it was. I also had no clue how to continue the conversation, but he had plenty of ideas.

Carter: I'm curious. Do you just like to read, or are you into all of this?

Holy shit, if I'd thought I was burning before... well now, he'd unleashed an inferno inside of me. Even my fingertips felt on fire as I typed.

Val: I can't believe you're asking this.

Carter: You promised we'd exchange notes.

Carter: On second thought, I'd rather hear the answer in person. I can't wait.

I stared at his message, then stared some more before laughter bubbled out of me. He was going to be the death of me. I didn't know if I should be afraid of it or look forward to it.

On Thursday afternoon, I went home a little early as my commitment for that evening was canceled. It was for the best because I was exhausted. I had a chance to catch up on some housework, as well as relax a little. I filled my tub with water and an unscented bubble lotion. After being nose-deep in samples all week, I needed a break from any kind of fragrance.

I propped a wooden tray across the tub, laying my Kindle, the phone, and a glass of water on it. Then I lit three candles and switched off the light. I sighed as I slid in the warm water, careful not to move the wooden table. This was heaven in a tub. If there was a better way to relax, I hadn't found it yet. I didn't even want to read, honestly. All I wanted was to close my eyes and let the exhaustion drip from my bones. I didn't even want to think about tomorrow. It was going to be a long day. But I was looking forward to dinner with my family... and the breakfast delivery.

As if sensing that I was thinking about him, Carter sent me a message.

Carter: Are you still at the office?

Val: At home already.

It was nearing eight o'clock, and I was

surprised that he was still at work. He usually messaged me after he left, and he was always out earlier than I was.

Carter: Damn. I wanted to pay you a surprise visit. You know, we still haven't set a date. When are you free for dinner?"

I swallowed. Oh... that. Before I could even reply, dots appeared on the screen. Carter was typing. I wanted to wait and see what else he had to say first.

Carter: I'm dying to taste you again. I'm attracted to you, Val. Not just on a physical level. I like how your mind works. I wanted to surprise you by whisking you to dinner tonight - no expectations. But since you're already home... how about tomorrow?

Val: I have dinner with my family tomorrow. But I have time every evening next week except Wednesday and Friday.

I waited with bated breath for his reply.

Carter: Do you have any plans tonight?

Val: Supreme relaxation. No bribe is high enough to get me out of my house.

Not five seconds later, my phone rang. I didn't pick it up from the tray, just activated the loudspeaker.

"You didn't think I'd give up easily, right?"

It was the first time I'd heard his voice this week, and it was even sexier than I remembered.

"It's your prerogative to try your best, but I'm warning you. I'm taking a hot bath. Nothing can top that."

"You're in a tub?"

"Yes."

A pause and then, "Why do you have your phone with you?"

"I have this fancy wooden tray that I use as support for stuff. Phone, Kindle, drink. I usually listen to music, and all of it is on my phone."

"You're naked right now?"

"I don't make it a habit to take baths fully clothed, so yes."

Now that he'd mentioned it, this did feel a little... erotic. Hearing his voice while I was stark naked, surrounded by the romantic light of the candles. This was my happy place. I usually set my phone in airplane mode, only using it to listen to music. But I was happy I hadn't switched it tonight.

"Val...."

Oh God, the way he'd said my name. He'd almost groaned it, as if it was a primal reaction to picturing me naked. The sound sent heat spiraling right to my clit.

"If I didn't know better, I'd say you want to punish me for something." His voice was deeper.

"I want to do no such thing. I'm just relaxing." Shit, my voice was breathy too.

"You deserve the time out."

"Thanks. I love this. It's like my private spa."

"You don't like going to an actual spa? With your sisters, or girlfriends?"

"I do, but I'm more of a DIY girl, even for manicures and so on. I don't like feeling strangers' hands on me. I went for a massage once. It was weird. I didn't enjoy it at all."

He gave a low laugh that sounded suspiciously like he was trying to cover up a groan.

"I'd give you a massage if I were with you. Trust me, you'd enjoy mine. I would touch you so good. Just where you need it."

My body was already on edge, anticipation building up as if he was just behind the door.

"Maybe I wouldn't want one," I replied playfully.

"Oh, I'd convince you. Wear you down."

"Is that so? And how would you do that?"

"I'll keep my secrets for now. But I think your imagination can fill in the blanks. Have a good night, Val."

"You too."

Holy hell, did my imagination ever flare up after the line went dead. I played music, then I sank into the tub up to my chin, grinning to myself, even though worry nagged at me. I liked that he'd said no expectations. It took off any pressure.

But I already felt a connection to Carter, and it was a little scary.

I was shaking my hips lightly to the rhythm of the slow music, but I wanted a more energetic sound. I hadn't selected a playlist, just let it shuffle around, and some slow songs had hijacked my evening. I set to rectifying the issue immediately. After drying my hands on a towel I kept nearby, I switched to my favorite playlist, and my mood immediately changed.

Oh, yeah.

With a jolt, I noticed Carter had sent me another message.

Carter: How about next Tuesday? I'm not giving up until we set a date in stone tonight.

I had just cooled down from our previous exchange, but now I felt as if someone had poured hot water in the tub.

Val: Next Tuesday works great.

Dots appeared on my screen, and my entire body was pulsing as I waited for his answer.

Carter: Perfect. I'll call you tomorrow to talk about the details. I won't hijack your naked time anymore... tonight.

Chapter Fourteen
Val

The next evening, mayhem reigned during Friday dinner.

I'd cooked chicken fajitas with iceberg salad on the side, and I'd monopolized my niece, Willow, holding her on my lap throughout dinner. I loved her toddler smell and the way she grabbed the fabric of my dress in her tiny fists.

"You, my dear, have excellent taste in clothing," I informed her, then asked no one in particular, "Is it too early to buy her scarves?"

My sisters were shoe lovers, but scarves were my kryptonite.

"Landon, watch your daughter," Jace cautioned, "or Val will turn her into a shopaholic."

"What's wrong with that?" Maddie asked, looking at her daughter happily. My twin had been a widower when he'd met her. I hadn't thought he would fall in love again. I was so grateful that Landon had found Maddie.

"She's a Connor girl," Landon said lazily. "I bet she was born with the shopping bug."

"That's my twin."

I was on a mission to discover if Jace was in

trouble. He and Hailey had their heads together again, chatting a little apart from the rest of the group. What was up with that? And Jace even had a few deep frown lines.

As the youngest, they always stuck together. If it was meant to be a secret, the joke was on him, because Hailey had the worst track record as secret keeper in the family.

After dinner, we chilled in the backyard, soaking the last sunrays. The evening was splendid. Under the guise of bringing out lemonade glasses for everyone, I roped my sisters into helping me.

"What's up with Jace?" I asked Hailey straight away. "You two have been whispering the whole evening. Last Friday too."

Hailey shook her head, making a gesture as if to indicate her lips were sealed.

"I've got nothing to say."

I exchanged a glance with Lori and could tell she was thinking the same thing. Since when did Hailey keep family secrets? It looked as if I'd have to actually put some effort into this. Huh... this was new.

"But speaking of secrets, you've been holding out on us, sister." Hailey spoke while she pressed lemons.

"Me?" I asked innocently.

Lori grinned. "We've been watching you. Twice you slipped in daydreaming mode, which you only do when you've had a great date or are planning one."

As a wedding planner, Lori caught on to these things quickly.

I looked from Lori to Hailey, and then the words burst out of me while I busied myself preparing a mix of honey and ginger. And because I didn't do anything halfheartedly, I went into great detail about the sexy time on the yacht, which caused Lori's cheeks to turn red. Hailey was eating it all up.

"Holy shit, way to go, sis. Oh, you so deserve a man who knows what he's doing," Hailey said.

"I do, don't I?" I said smugly. "We're having dinner next week."

"Why not the weekend?" Hailey asked.

"He's busy with his nieces."

After we returned outside, I moved on to the second part of the plan: cornering Jace.

I just hoped he hadn't picked up on the daydreaming vibes my sister had. After the fiasco with Ethan, Jace was even more protective.

Those protective instincts had reared their heads for the first time when he was thirteen and he'd grilled a guy who'd come to pick up Lori for a date like it was his job. When I had asked him about it, he'd simply said, "When a guy at my school goes to pick up girls on dates, the girl's dad always gives them shit. Dad isn't here, so I'll do it."

I'd been so stunned that I'd even forgotten to scold him for saying shit. My thirteen-year-old brother was growing up far too fast, and I hadn't known how to stop it. And now he was a grown man I was proud of. But if he was in trouble, I wanted to know. I wasn't just trying to be nosy. I could help.

I'd arranged lounge chairs throughout the yard. Lori's husband, Graham, was sitting with their son, Milo, on Jace's left. Graham owned the soccer club where Jace played, and while the boys tried not to talk shop during family dinners, they sometimes got into heated discussions about the games.

I took the chair to Jace's right.

"Brother dearest, it has come to my attention that you're keeping secrets with Hailey."

Jace looked at Hailey in alarm, but our sister shook her head. Jace grinned at me.

"If Hailey managed to keep quiet, you seriously think I'll spill the beans?"

"What if I promise to cook your favorite next week? As a proof of affection. And you could show some gratitude in advance."

I batted my eyelashes, going for the deer-caught-in-the-headlights look that Lori pulled off so well and that worked like a charm on Jace. Unfortunately, I sucked at it. All I managed was to make Jace laugh.

"Nice try, Val. Nice try."

***

A cappuccino, a pancake, and yogurt with muesli. I grinned as I took inventory of my delivered breakfast on Monday, then shot Carter a message.

Val: Any particular reason you've been extra generous today?

Carter: Setting the mood for tomorrow.

My heart rate sped up as I dug into my food. I could tell I wasn't going to be very productive today, but I was allowed to daydream once in a while, wasn't I?

I was ecstatic right until shortly before lunchtime, when I was served papers. Everything inside me froze when I saw the sender was Beauty SkinEssence.

I willed myself not to be jittery as I signed for the papers, but then my legs turned into Jell-O. I didn't make it to my desk. Instead, I leaned against the wall next to the door and pulled out the documents.

They were suing me.

My heart sank. I read through the details, absorbing them.

Then I did something I hadn't done in a long while. I closed the door to my office before sitting in the chair behind my desk, feeling drained of all energy. I'd prepared for this scenario, of course. I'd just hoped it wouldn't occur. It would require a lot of time and money I could use elsewhere. An inkling of doubt set in. Had I been stupid not to settle during mediation? But killing the line would have effectively meant admitting guilt, and I simply couldn't have lived with that. But now, when faced point-blank with the result, I wondered if swallowing my pride was the best course of action. I'd worked my ass off for so long to get where I was, to bring the company to a point where it was solid and profitable, and now this.

I willed myself to ignore the tight knot in my stomach, but I couldn't. What if the litigation ended up at trial? What if the judge ruled against me? What if I lost more than this line? God, there I went again, overthinking everything.

But I couldn't help it. The company was so tied to who I was. I still remembered that euphoric feeling I'd had when Landon and I signed the papers for incorporating. I'd wanted to build something everyone could be proud of: me, my parents, and Landon too. I'd also wanted to prove to myself that I could make my dream come true. I wouldn't let anyone take it away from me.

I wasn't sure how long I'd been locked inside by myself, mulling over everything, and wishing the day would just end so I could go home and sink in my tub. I heard a knock at my door.

"Val, everything all right?" Anne asked. "You have a meeting in ten minutes."

"I'll be on time."

I checked my phone. I'd been wallowing for twenty minutes. And I had a new message from Carter.

Carter: Do you have time for lunch?

I typed a message, then deleted it, then typed another one.

Val: No. My day just got a lot worse :((I have to go into a meeting right now.

Carter: Did something happen?

I sent him a picture of the papers. Carter

didn't answer right away, and I didn't have time to wait. I rushed into the meeting, leaving my phone behind, not wanting to be distracted.

I forced myself to focus because the gentlemen had flown in from Italy. They produced some of the rarest essences, and I wanted to strike a deal with them.

The meeting lasted longer than I'd hoped, and by the time we'd finalized the details, I was light-headed. I hadn't eaten since breakfast, and it was almost four o'clock. I walked the gentlemen to the elevator, and the second the door slid to a close, I turned to Anne.

"Can you get me something to eat? Anything at all."

"Sure, boss. But you've got someone waiting in your office for you."

"Oh? I didn't have any other meeting on my calendar."

"A Carter Sloane dropped by unannounced. Said he had to talk to you. He's been waiting for an hour. Couldn't get rid of him."

"Of course not. Thanks for the heads-up. I'll talk to him. But please, hurry with that sandwich, or I'll faint."

Anne darted to the elevator as I spun on my heels, heading to my office. My empty stomach rolled over. When I reached the doorway to my office, Carter rose to his feet. I tried to read his body language but was too tired and hungry to make much headway.

"Anne said you've been waiting for an hour."

He held up his phone. "You didn't answer my text or call."

"I was in a meeting."

"I know, Anne told me. Called the office when you weren't answering."

I stepped inside, closing the door again.

Chapter Fifteen
Val

"Let's get out of here," Carter said. "I heard what you said to Anne about the sandwich. I'll feed you, and you relax and don't think about any of this."

I placed my hands on my hips. "You can't just barge in here and take charge."

His eyes flashed. The corners of his mouth twitched.

"Yes, I can, especially if you need it."

Well, how could I argue with that? I was dying for time out.

"It's early."

"It's four o'clock, and you told Anne that you don't have any other meetings today."

"Doesn't mean I don't have anything else to do."

"You own this business. You can't give yourself a few hours off?"

"How about you? Don't you have to clock every hour?"

"I cleared off my schedule."

The fight went right out of me because I distinctly remembered he'd had meetings into the evening today. It was the reason we were supposed to go out tomorrow.

He picked my bag from my desk and my jacket from the hanger, holding both out for me. The man was unbelievable, but the fact that he'd taken the afternoon off and was here for me disarmed me faster than I would have thought possible. I let him slide the jacket on my back. He lingered with his fingers at the sides of my neck, pressing gently. I released an audible breath.

"Come on, Val. I'll take your mind off it." He lowered his hand to the small of my back and kept it there on the way to the elevator. We ran into Anne as we headed out of the building.

"You're leaving?" she inquired as she handed me the sandwich.

"Yes, but call me if anything urgent comes up."

"Okay. I'll see you tomorrow."

After she left, Carter pointed to the sandwich.

"This is supposed to be your lunch?"

I nodded, too busy devouring the tiny turkey sandwich to answer. He was right, though. It was so small that I finished it just as we went out of the building. I felt even hungrier than before.

"What do you want to do?" he asked.

I blinked. "You bossed me out of my own office, and now you're asking me what I want to do?"

"The important thing was to get you out. You were so tense that your shoulders were up to your ears. I can make dinner reservations, but I'm sensing you're not up to it."

He came to a stop on the sidewalk, and I stopped too. God, no one had looked at me the way he did. What would it feel like to have this man inside me? To have him in my life? Would he make me feel things no one else had?

"Honestly, I just want to go home."

"Then that's where we'll go."

"We?"

"You don't honestly think I'd let you go on your own?" He cupped my face gently, caressing my cheeks with his thumbs. "Let me be with you today, okay?"

I sighed and nodded, already looking forward to it. He didn't immediately let go of my face, and I started to warm up at all those contact points. My eyes were at the same level with his lips. I remembered how they'd felt on my skin. A current of awareness passed through me. The look in Carter's eyes told me he knew exactly what was going through my mind. Sexual tension filled every single inch of distance between us. I was lost in this man: his touch, the seductive tone of his voice. When he let go of me, I immediately missed him.

We drove in separate cars, and every time I peeked in the rearview mirror to check if he was still tailing me, my heart sighed.

There were no major traffic jams, so we arrived at my house in no time. We locked eyes as we climbed out of our respective cars.

"Welcome to my home." I pushed open the

gate, and then climbed the stone steps in my yard.

"This yard is fantastic," he commented.

"I know. I love it."

Carter brought a hand to my back, and I felt as if the contact was skin to skin. All the messaging this past week had felt like foreplay, and now my entire body was so responsive to that one small touch that I was ashamed.

"Want a tour?" I asked nervously once we were inside.

"Sure."

I showed him the ground floor quickly, and then the upper floor. I could feel myself becoming jittery.

"I don't have any food in the fridge, but we could order something, even though it takes ages for delivery in this part of the city."

"We'll figure it out."

As I was showing him the master bathroom with my beloved tub, Carter brought a hand to my chin, tilting it up.

"What do you do when you come home to relax?"

"I take a shower and change in comfy clothes. Or... I walk around naked. My dad liked to say 'your sweatpants will never be tight if you don't wear any,' and that's one of my favorite sayings."

"Let's make a deal. I'll run to that small convenience store up the street, buy some food. You shower and relax."

My pulse went from zero to holy hell in two

seconds. I chose to concentrate on the neutral part of the sentence.

"They don't have a lot of options."

"I'll make do. Don't think about it. Stay here and relax. But do put on clothes after your shower. We can try the no-sweatpants thing another time."

I couldn't tell if he was inviting himself into the shower or not, but my pulse was erratic now. He stroked his thumb over my lips, and then his mouth captured mine. My knees weakened from the first stroke of his tongue.

My clit throbbed, and my nipples turned hard as if they were anxious for his tongue too.

"I've been dying to kiss you all week," he murmured before diving in for a second kiss. This one was hotter, more urgent. I rose on my tiptoes, gripping his shoulders for leverage as I feverishly kissed him back. I became aware that both of his hands were on my waist, and he was walking me backward until my back was against the wall. The tiles felt cold even through the fabric of my dress, and my hips arched forward. He was so close that I slammed my lower body right into his, and sweet heavens, his hard-on was impressive.

A groan tore from him, and then he took a step back.

"Now, now. Be a good girl and relax."

He winked and left the bathroom. I was so worked up that I almost called him right back to demand more of those scorching-hot kisses.

Then I decided to focus on the shower. I

pushed down my clothes, and I became more worked up with each layer I took off. I showered quickly, then rubbed my favorite body cream on my skin, wrapped a towel around myself, and headed to my bedroom. I sank into the leather armchair opposite my bed, hoisting my legs up on the ottoman and just allowing my body to cool down and the cream to sink in.

I'd left the door cracked open, figuring it was the only way I'd hear if Carter needed something when he returned from the store, and grinned when I heard him singing a while later. Oh, hell. That sexy man was singing in my kitchen, and I was missing the show?

Forget the bubble bath, that would be the utmost relaxation. Watching him… and possibly climbing right into his arms.

No, no. I had my instructions. I couldn't deny it. It was fun not to know what was about to happen.

Sometime later, I heard footsteps coming up the stairs, and the muscles in my belly strummed together.

"I'm in the bedroom," I announced.

Was he coming inside?

Yes, yes, he was.

My breath hitched when he appeared in the doorway, looking all enticing and holding a plate with a sandwich.

He placed it on the small table next to the armchair.

I didn't miss the way his eyes roamed over the

length of my body. A towel covered me, but I was still stark naked underneath it, and my nipples tightened when his gaze focused on them.

I salivated at the sight of the sandwich with slices of avocado and ham and quickly took a bite, then let out a long sigh. "This is delicious."

He perched on the edge of the armchair, watching me intently. I was pretending to keep my eyes on the food, but I wasn't doing a great job. The air seemed to thicken with sexual tension with every minute we spent together in this intimate setting, and I wasn't sure I could take it any longer.

"This is my reading armchair," I informed him.

"I see. So this is where you read all those scandalous books."

"Yep."

As I downed the last bite, Carter clasped one of my ankles. I felt his touch all the way up to my inner thighs. Our eyes locked. I swallowed, aware that I was breathing faster.

"What are you doing?" I asked.

"You'll see."

Bliss. Pure and utter bliss. He massaged my foot, applying pressure on the arch and on the pads, then on each toe.

He moved his hand a little further up my ankle before returning it to caress my heel. Then he switched to the other sole. His fingers were pure magic... and he was turning me on. Did a foot massage count as foreplay? Everything felt like foreplay with him.

"Tell me what you're thinking."

I licked my lips, unsure if honesty was the best policy right now because my thoughts were so far past X-rated, they deserved their own rating.

"That bad, huh? It's okay. I know exactly what you're thinking."

"And how do you know?" I teased.

"I can read body language very well. Our bodies usually betray us." He wiggled his eyebrows, and I felt myself blush even more.

"But you can't see anything."

He lowered my foot back on the ottoman, then slid closer to me, placing my plate on the small table.

There was nothing between us now, and when Carter leaned in to kiss me, I pushed myself up, fully aware that my towel was sliding down and my breasts were on display.

God, the man kissed like no other. He buried one hand in my hair, tilting my head while he ravished me with his lips and tongue.

I needed his touch desperately. My body was begging for it.

Chapter Sixteen
Carter

I slid my hand down from her hair to her neck, and then to her breasts. She arched into my touch, moaning in my mouth. She was beautiful, all worked up like this for me. I slid my hand even lower and rubbed two fingers over her pussy, from her clit down to her entrance.

She moaned louder, gripping at my shirt with both hands when I removed her towel completely. I was going to make this woman come. I wanted to give her so much pleasure that I'd rock her world. She opened her thighs wider, allowing me access. I rubbed up and down her opening, alternating between touching her clit and teasing her inner thighs, working her up. And all the while, I couldn't stop kissing her. I wanted to watch her beautiful face, but I needed to taste her. When I slid one finger inside her, Val's entire body shook.

Then she unhitched her mouth from mine just for a few seconds, long enough to say, "Another one. Pleaaaase."

I thought I might burst in my pants. I kissed her again, sliding in a second finger, and then we were both out of control. I moved my fingers in and out, curving them to hit her sweet spot, stroking her clit with my thumb. This wasn't enough. I couldn't touch her the way I wanted in this position. I couldn't taste her. So I withdrew my hand, laughing when she closed her thighs to try and trap me there.

"Come closer, baby. I want to taste you."

She let out a small whimper as I pulled her to the edge of the armchair. I was on my knees and placed her thighs on my shoulders. When I pressed my tongue against her sensitive flesh, she cried out my name.

"Carter! Oh, fuck."

I was shaking with need while I pushed my tongue inside, twirling it, driving her crazy. I'd worked her up so well that she wouldn't last long. When I felt that she was close, I moved my mouth to her clit, sliding two fingers inside her again, curving them. She exploded beautifully, and I went up to pull her close and hold her as she rode the waves of pleasure. I rocked her in my arms, inhaling the fruity scent of her hair, caressing the soft skin on her shoulders.

Then she traced a straight line with her finger along my shirt buttons, stopping at my belt. She unfastened it and lowered my zipper, freeing my cock.

"Baby," I whispered as she stroked my erection once, then took me in her mouth. I didn't last long either. I'd wanted her for so long that I tipped past the edge within minutes.

"You're gorgeous," I whispered when she reached for her towel, which I'd dropped to the floor. "Allow me."

I took the towel from her and patted her skin, starting from her ankles, all the way up.

"My skin is not dry enough for you?" she asked with a smirk. She didn't have one drop of water on her.

"Nope."

I took a detour when I reached her inner thighs, licking once across her center. Then another detour when I was drying off her breasts, pulling each nipple in my mouth. I was getting hard again.

All I wanted to do was flip her around and bend her over. But I didn't know if she was ready for all that yet.

"Let's go downstairs," I suggested while I was kissing her neck.

"I don't like that idea." A second later, I registered that she was unbuttoning my shirt.

"Val, baby...."

I straightened up to look at her, and those beautiful green eyes were full of desire. I slid my hands to cup her ass and lifted her in my arms. She whimpered with anticipation as she wrapped her long legs around me. I carried her to the bed, lowering her on it. I could hardly hear anything past the thumping in my ears. I wanted this woman more than I'd ever wanted anything.

When I lowered her on the bed, she attempted to close her knees.

"No, stay like this. Spread wide for me. I want to watch you while I take off my clothes."

Her eyes flared, but she kept her legs where they were. I'd never gotten naked faster. Then I remembered one small detail....

"My wallet is downstairs. I have a condom there."

Val licked her lips. "I'm on the pill, and I'm healthy."

I leaned on the bed over her, feathering my lips on her jaw. "I'm healthy too, but...baby, you want me bare inside you?"

She nodded, and I wrapped her in my arms, kissing her. Our release just before had been satisfying but quick. I wanted this to last. I kissed down her collarbone, then I flipped her onto her belly, touching my lips to her spine until I reached her tailbone. She moaned when I kissed her right ass cheek, covering the left one with my palm before I pushed a finger inside her. She was wet and ready, but I wanted to drive her crazy with anticipation first, so I flipped her around again and skimmed my lips right over her pussy. Then I gave her my tongue.

I held her pelvis up at the angle I needed it, making her dig her heels deep into the mattress and grope at the sheets. I was lying flat on my front, and my cock was wedged between my body and the mattress. It was almost painful. When her breathing became too labored, I turned to explore the rest of her body. Her inner thighs, her breasts, until our faces were level.

She looked at me as if I was everything to her. I kissed her deeply while I positioned my erection between her thighs. Val moaned when I gave her the tip.

Oh, fuck, fuck, fuck.

There was no feeling in the world comparable to being inside this woman, to feeling her snug around me without any barriers. I pushed inside inch by inch, watching her beautiful face crumple with pleasure. She opened up her thighs wider, drawing her knees up. I drove into her, my pelvis pushing against hers. We were both relentless, chasing our release. But when I felt I was too close, I pulled out, bringing my lips to her ear.

"On your hands and knees."

Val complied, and through a haze of lust, she turned. I kneaded her ass cheeks, kissing up her back as I slid inside her, fast and hard. I had easy access to her clit in this position, and I circled it, spurring her to tremors. Then she moved her hands from the bed to grip the headboard. She had better leverage like this, and she slammed into me with the same hunger I was pushing inside her. Her arms were trembling slightly, as if her body couldn't take any more pleasure.

When she started clenching around me, calling out my name, I was completely done for. I came hard, holding on to her. Her legs shook even after she climaxed, and I cocooned my body around hers, propping my thighs outside hers, keeping an arm around her waist and my chest pressed against her back. I was kissing what I could reach of her neck, needing as much contact as possible.

"Are you okay, beautiful?"

Her breath was ragged, but she chuckled. "I'm still recovering."

After we showered, she wrapped a towel around herself.

"Oh, hell, no. You are putting on actual clothes."

"Or what?"

"Or I'll eat you instead of dinner."

She grinned. "I don't think I'd mind."

"Come on, tempting girl. Put on some clothes."

Pouting, she complied, heading to her bedroom.

"I don't have a T-shirt big enough for you," she called. "But if you want to walk around shirtless, I won't mind."

"Should I just not put on clothes at all?"

"You won't hear me complain about that."

I didn't put my shirt on in the end, because I needed to let it dry. Watching Val peek at me while we were bustling about the kitchen gave me a lot of satisfaction. For once, she was the one at a disadvantage.

"You were singing earlier," she commented.

"Really? I didn't notice." I didn't usually sing, Val had this effect on me—I was extremely relaxed and also extremely turned on around her. Val arranged the sandwiches I'd made on two plates at the counter.

I massaged her shoulder blades, partly because they were still a bit hunched, and partly because I couldn't keep my hands off her.

"You're still a little tense."

"Yeah."

"Do you want to talk about it?"

"Not really. My lawyer will handle it. I've discussed all the options with him; I had just hoped it wouldn't come to it."

"How good is he?"

"My lawyer?"

"Yes."

"He's one of the best." She gave me his name, and I wasn't too happy. He was good, but I was better.

"What if I took your case?"

She turned around, her eyes widening before she shook her head. "No, that's not a good idea."

"Why not? I'm a very good lawyer—"

"I don't doubt that, but I think it's smarter to separate our professional and personal lives."

She looked down, and I got the hint. In case things between us didn't work out, it was easier if we kept the two spheres separate. I understood the message. A vein pulsed in my temple. I didn't like it one bit, but I understood it.

"Val, I want to be honest with you. Whenever I'm with you, it just feels surreal. This past week, I've thought more about you than anything else. I know my life isn't easy, but I'd like for us to enjoy this between us. As I said before, without expectations. You said you want to take things easy and I respect that."

Her eyes searched mine for a few seconds. I could give her what she wanted. Easy fit well in the whirlwind of obligations that was my life. Being in this woman's house, surrounded by her, gave me a glimpse of who she was. Her warmth reached all the way inside me, and I felt alive in a way I hadn't before.

When she rose on her tiptoes and pressed her lips to mine, I swear something melted inside of me.

"Hell, yes. Now come on, mister. Show me your massage talents."

She laughed as I carried the plates to the table.

"You're doubting me?"

"No at all. I know some of your other talents, and I can't wait to discover all of them."

To prove her wrong, I stood behind her as she ate the second sandwich, working the pressure points of her neck and shoulders.

"Oh, this is so good. Dinner, and your hands. Aren't you hungry?"

I brought my mouth to her ear. "Not for food, no."

She sucked in a deep breath, pressing her thighs together.

"Well, I think you should eat anyway."

"Why, are my hands distracting you?"

"Maybe."

"Impressed with my massage skills, I take it?"

She sighed. "Yes, yes I am. What other skills do you possess? Just so I'm prepared."

"I'll keep them a secret for now."

"Wait a second, you've been inside me and you're gonna keep secrets?"

I sat next to her, playing with a few strands of her hair. "Before I divulge anything, I need to be inside you a couple more times. See your beautiful face when I make you come."

She swallowed, and I nearly boosted her up on the table. My appetite for this woman was insatiable. I kissed her exposed shoulders, moving from one to the other, enjoying how it made her squirm. We chatted leisurely during dinner, and after we were done, we moved to her couch. I pulled her feet into my lap, massaging her arches.

"I'm going to make dessert," she said after a while, half rising from the couch before I pulled her back and she plopped right into my lap.

"Val, come here."

"Why?"

"I want to hold you for a bit." I inhaled her sweet scent, touching her neck with the tip of my nose. "I'm glad you've agreed to bring me here with you tonight."

"As I recall, I didn't have much of a choice."

"I forgot that detail." I smiled, kissing her jaw, then her earlobe. After I let her go, she skidded to the kitchen, whipping up a smoothie that tasted delicious. I couldn't stop touching her no matter what she did. So when we returned to the couch, I pulled her right in my lap again. Her thighs were at my sides, and I nibbled on her neck.

"What are you doing?" she inquired.

"I'm about to thank you for the dessert." I kissed her collarbone, then pushed her strapless dress down, to have access to her breasts. When I sucked a nipple in my mouth, she rewarded me with a delicious moan.

"And how are you going to do that?"

"I have a few ideas."

Chapter Seventeen
Val

"Ms. Connor, I like what I'm hearing. I've been keeping an eye on your company for a few years, and I believe your products are a great fit for our clients." Davis spoke in a low, even voice.

"I'm glad to hear that."

I smiled politely, even though I was doing an inner dance. I'd worked for years to get his attention. He was the founder of one of the biggest perfume-only chains in California that sold high-end fragrances. I hadn't believed my luck when he'd called to set up a meeting. I'd met him for lunch at one of my favorite restaurants near my office, and I couldn't help sweeping my gaze across the terrace, hoping to catch a glimpse of Carter. He said he'd eat here with a group. I'd met my lawyer on Tuesday evening last week, so we hadn't gone out on a date yet... but we had tentative plans for tonight. And we'd had lunch together every day for the past week and a half.

"It's mid-November, so we won't catch the Christmas rush, but in the new year we could start by featuring one of your trademark lines like the Dreamsetter, and after we see how it performs, we could potentially talk about an exclusive line like the one you have for Sephora."

"You know about it?"

"A man like me doesn't come to a meeting without doing his due diligence. You have a fresh perspective. Not corporate, nor artisan. You're somewhere in between, and that's what we're looking for."

"You did feature a few artisan lines though."

"We tried that route, even though I was against it from the beginning. Artisans have the craft in mind first and foremost, not the consumer, and that is reflected in sales. But you, Ms. Connor, have found your niche and you did very well for yourself."

Davis smiled shrewdly from under his bushy, pearl-white mustache. Being complimented by a business legend like him was high praise indeed.

"Would you like to go by my office afterward? I could show you some of our current top-secret projects."

"Thank you for the offer, but I'm heading straight to LAX from here. However, I'm going to put you in touch with my grandson. He handles the field work, so to speak. I'm sure you two will hit it off."

"Sure."

We chitchatted about the latest trends in fragrances, which were likely to last and which would be summer fads. We were halfway through our lunch when I saw Carter walk in with a large group. He winked at me before choosing to sit in a chair from which he had a direct view of me.

I winked back as discreetly as possible, then focused on Davis, continuing our conversation. I felt Carter looking at me, though. Out of the corner of my eye, I spied on him from time to time, and every single time, he met my gaze. Did the man not care that the others at the table could notice? Evidently not. I felt very flattered by that... but all those scorching-hot gazes he was sending me were messing with my focus. I trained my attention on my future business partner, who was now telling me all about his grandson and how he'd groomed him to take over when he retired because his son had no interest.

I was doing so well, concentrating on our small talk, ignoring those scorching-hot looks a certain someone was sending me. But then my phone pinged with an incoming message. I had it on the table, out of habit, and saw the message.

Carter: I've missed you.

It was bad form to answer, so I tried to ignore it, but something fluttered in my belly. A second message arrived a few minutes later.

Carter: You're a knockout in those clothes. I can't wait to take them off you.

The flutters migrated south. I pressed my thighs together on reflex. Oh, Carter. Where were his manners now? Seducing me when I was in the middle of a business lunch.

I discreetly pushed the phone away and even more discreetly sent Carter a glare across the restaurant. The joke was on me when a few minutes later, the screen of my phone lit up with another message. I couldn't see it, and I was dying to know what it said.

I clasped my hands together to keep myself from reaching the phone. When lunch ended, Davis asked for the bill.

"It's my treat," I said.

"Oh, no, no, no. When an old man like me goes out with a young lady, he never lets her pay."

"I insist. I was the one who wanted to meet at a restaurant."

He chuckled. "Fiery. I can't wait for my grandson to meet you. He's quite a fiery personality himself."

I squinted my eyes. Was he trying to set us up?

"You'd make a great pair."

Oh my God, he was. I laughed at his brazen attitude but wasn't surprised. Davis was known for doing things his way and not caring one bit about business protocol.

We shook hands as we stood up, and I glanced at the screen of my smartphone before slipping it into my purse.

Carter: Meet me inside the restaurant after you're done.

I lifted my gaze just enough to see Carter rise from his chair and leave the terrace, heading into the building.

After bidding Davis goodbye, I followed Carter inside. My heart was thundering in my chest, as if I was about to do something illicit.

Even though it was pleasantly cool inside, the restaurant was empty, since all patrons had chosen to eat on the terrace. I felt Carter's presence before even noticing him. I knew he was watching me before I turned on my heels and spotted him in the far corner, in a nook of sorts. He smiled at me, and I swear, I felt a zing everywhere on my skin. I headed right to him, attempting to sound stern.

"You can't do this."

"What?"

"Distract me like this during business hours."

He lifted one corner of his mouth. "You were having lunch."

"A business lunch."

"Come here."

Before I could even reply, he tugged me by the waist, bringing me close. His mouth came down on mine the next second. He licked my lower lip before biting it slightly. I felt the touch straight on the tips of my breasts and pressed myself against him as he deepened the kiss.

"We're in a restaurant," I whispered afterward. "Did you forget your manners?"

"You make me forget even my damn name, Val." He spoke against my lips, twirling strands of hair between his fingers. "I wasn't joking when I said I missed you."

"So that was why you were sending me hot texts during my business meal? Because you missed me?"

"Wasn't the only reason. Wanted to remind you that I wasn't far away, in case old Davis was too charming."

"Don't worry. He was just complimenting my business skills."

"You're going to work together?"

"Looks like it. He was even talking about the possibility of an exclusive line."

"That's great, babe. I'm happy for you. Will you be working directly with him?"

"No, he mentioned that he's grooming his grandson to take over." On a chuckle, I added, "I think he's hoping we'll hit it off. Said we'd make a good pair."

Carter's smile fell. His jaw tightened, and he looked at me strangely, then cast his gaze away.

"And what about you?" he asked eventually.

I was confused.

"What about me?"

"Are you hoping you'll hit it off?"

"Well, I certainly hope he'll be as impressed as his grandfather."

"I didn't mean in the boardroom."

I furrowed my brow. "I don't understand."

"Do you want to go out with him?" I'd never heard him sound so strained.

"What? No, of course not." My stomach knotted, wondering where exactly this conversation was going. We hadn't explicitly set boundaries, but I had to know exactly where we stood... I couldn't make the mistake of assuming again.

He cupped one side of my face, tilting my head back, running his thumb over my lower lip. "I don't want you to go out with anyone else."

I let out a breath of relief. "I won't. I ditched the guy who was supposed to be my date for the charity event because I discovered he hadn't wanted us to be exclusive but didn't bother to tell me."

"I'm sorry." Carter pulled back a notch, taking my hands in his and kissing each cheek before looking back up at me.

He smiled lazily, feathering his lips over mine. "But I want to make one thing clear, Val. You're the only woman I even think about."

I didn't think he knew how much those words meant to me. They made me feel valued and important, not like an afterthought. He smiled, bringing our interlaced hands up to the sides of my face. Next thing I knew, he kissed me so heatedly that I nearly climbed him right there in the restaurant.

"Carter, what if someone comes in?" I admonished.

"They'll look the other way."

"Isn't your party waiting for you outside?"

"I don't really give a fuck." He spoke in a raw voice. "Blow off the rest of your day."

"I can't. You can't."

"Try me." He rained kisses on my cheek, moving to my ear. "I want to prove to you how much you've been on my mind. To show you exactly what I want to do to you."

LAYLA HAGEN

Oh, God. I was so close to saying yes and forgetting everything on my to-do list. But I somehow managed to gather my wits.

"Nope. You, sir, have distracted me enough today. Go back to work and stop corrupting me."

"I'll see you at six, then."

We hadn't made any plans beyond catching up, so I tilted my head, deciding to play with him. "I have a meeting starting late in the afternoon, so I need a rain check."

"Are you fucking with me?" The words came out on a growl, which made me giggle. "You are."

"Yes, yes, I am. About the rain check. I do have a meeting late in the afternoon."

He trained that scorching hot gaze on me.

"Don't let it go overtime too much, or I'm going to barge in and throw you over my shoulder before it's over."

Chapter Eighteen
Val

I arrived back in the office and scowled as soon as I peeked at my agenda. My lawyer was coming in again to discuss the litigation.

"I've got everything prepared," he summed up after we went back and forth over the details for an hour.

"Good. Thank you for everything."

After he left, I took out the pink notebook I used for brainstorming catchphrases for marketing copy, but I couldn't concentrate. Instead, I found myself drawing a lilac plant—the key ingredient in the skincare line that Beauty SkinEssence wanted me to drop.

I was glad that I had the date with Carter to look forward to because otherwise I'd drive myself crazy with worry again. As the afternoon went by, though, I went into a bit of a frenzy.

I wasn't dressed for a date. I was wearing a peasant blouse and a maxi skirt. Usually, I would wear something more conservative for a business meeting, but Davis was known for being casual. He'd been wearing a Hawaiian shirt today.

Carter and I had only made plans for tonight

after I'd left my house, so I couldn't change.

That afternoon, I glanced at the clock more often than usual, willing time to pass more quickly, even though I was immersed in my favorite activity: sampling. At five thirty, I went into one of the bathrooms to freshen up, applying deodorant and some more mascara.

Then I whistled for no reason at all.

"Who has a date with a gorgeous man?" I sang. "That's right. Me."

I felt a little silly, but I was officially off the clock, so I could let my playful side come out.

"Who is going to have a great time? Me."

I was about to start shimmying my hips in a dance too, when I heard the water flush in one of the toilets and groaned inwardly.

Samantha, one of my accounting employees, came out. She was trying very hard to fight a smile. I greeted her, maintaining a poker face even though I could feel the tips of my ears heating up. Just my luck. But hey, I did have a gorgeous man coming to pick me up. One couldn't be lucky in everything.

While I waited for Carter in the lobby, I checked on Jace, who had returned from a game outside LA a few hours ago.

Val: Do you have any food? Did you sustain any injury?

Jace: No to both, but before you ask me to come by for dinner, I'm reminding you we've entered the era of home delivery. I'm going to go to bed right away and sleep for twelve hours straight, but I'll call you tomorrow, okay?

Val: Sure. Take care.

Eh, some habits were not easily shaken off. Of course, I knew that Jace didn't need all the doting, but I couldn't help it. I just hoped I wasn't getting on his nerves.

Will used to be a detective, and I constantly worried about him when he was on the force. I tried not to let it show, but I don't think I was doing a good job.

My brothers did indulge me, but sometimes I felt like one of those moms who made their grown-up children roll their eyes every time her name appeared on the screen of their phone.

Carter arrived then, and I licked my lips as he crossed the room to reach me. The man was simply a work of art. His hair was neat, and I couldn't wait to ruffle it up a bit. He raked his gaze over me, and I felt my body respond to him. My skin was burning for his touch.

"Ready to go?"

I nodded. Up close, he was even more alluring, with that top button open and his delicious scent surrounding me. I readjusted the strap of my bag on my shoulder, aware that he was still watching me intently, as if he was mentally undressing me.

"You look beautiful."

"Not dressed for a date, but I didn't have time to go home and change. I know my style is a bit... different."

"I like it. I like that you're different and you're not afraid to show it."

"Dad used to say 'if you can't hide the crazy, own it.'"

He came closer, placing a hand on my waist. His fingers were pressing in as if he could barely wait to touch me. He brought his mouth to mine, kissing me with so much fervor that I felt myself become slick between my legs. I pressed myself into him, needing more contact still. I was happy we were in a small nook of the lobby, hidden from sight.

Lord, the effect this man had on me should be outlawed. He rested his head in the crook of my neck.

"You drive me insane." He almost growled the words. "Let's go before I forget all about tonight's plans."

I smiled as we left the building, proud that I had this kind of effect on him.

"Dinner in the dark," I exclaimed forty minutes later when we arrived at the destination. I read the words on the menu displayed next to the entrance to the restaurant. "This is exciting."

I'd read about it. The food was served completely in the dark. The lack of light made the other senses sharper.

Once we were inside, a friendly waitress led us to a small separate room that was still bathed in light. I loved that the chairs were on adjacent sides of the table and not opposite each other. The waitress explained that the menu contained five courses, and we had to choose between three options for the main course.

Someone turned the lights off just before we were served the appetizers. It was remarkable how different the experience was, as if I wasn't simply dining, but having a sensory feast. I made a mental note to perform the sampling process with the lights turned off next time. I sometimes closed my eyes when I focused on a sample but wondered if the experience would be different. I couldn't wait to try it.

"I've always wanted to try something like this," I said.

"I thought you'd like it."

"Really? Why?"

"Because it's an unusual thing to do."

I squirmed in my seat. "I know I'm a bit odd. The way I dress, and how I pop out Dad's sayings every now and again."

I felt his hand cover mine. "Valentina, I meant it as a compliment. And I don't think it's odd at all that you use your dad's sayings so often. You're a very warm and loving person. It's your way of keeping his memory alive."

I'd never thought about it like that, but now that he said it, I knew it was true. I became more and more aware of him as he kept touching my hand. I had trouble concentrating on the main course because the man next to me captured my attention.

"And? Have I earned the right to know your

deep, dark secrets?" Carter asked.

"Hmm… I'd say you're getting closer."

"You're taking advantage." It was obvious from his tone that he was smiling. I liked this dinner-in-the-dark experience. It was fun guessing his reactions.

"You think? But I will say this: I haven't had so much fun since we were out on the boat."

"Well, that just confirms it. I'm the common denominator here."

I laughed, acutely aware that he was touching my leg under the table. The darkness made everything sexier.

"I'm glad you're having a good time."

"It's fun. And I feel so… free when I'm with you. Like I can just be myself."

He kissed my hand, and then he intertwined our fingers.

"Don't ever feel the need to pretend you're someone else. You're a remarkable woman, Valentina Connor."

"Thank you."

I sighed, wondering how on earth I was supposed to keep my expectations from building when he said things like these that, well… made me wish he'd be around for the long haul so he could keep saying them.

"April loves your style, by the way."

"What are you talking about? I wore a sundress on the yacht."

"She's been stalking your Facebook and

Instagram. She's made this list with everything she wants to buy. We're hitting stores this weekend. I'm already afraid."

"I can come with you and help," I offered.

"Thanks, but don't you worry about it. We'll do fine."

I cringed, closing my eyes, happy he couldn't see me. Why did I have to poke my nose in things all the time? I knew I could be a little too doting and overbearing. If he didn't invite me, I wasn't going to push the issue. Things had to progress naturally. You couldn't make someone want you in their life, no matter how much you tried. You couldn't love for two; I'd learned that the hard way over the years.

Carter put a hand on my thigh, moving his thumb in a gentle rubbing motion. I caught my breath.

"I can't wait to have you all to myself tonight." His voice was low and seductive. If I thought my senses had been heightened before, it was nothing compared to this. The skin under my skirt had turned to goose bumps, and an ache was settling between my thighs.

"You do have me all to yourself right now," I teased, knowing full well what he meant.

"I want to take off all your clothes and touch you right here." He moved his hand further up, close to the apex of my thigh. "Kiss you there too. Nip and lick."

A tremor coursed through me at the word lick. I felt Carter lean in next and place a kiss on my upper arm, then my shoulder. The moment was interrupted by the arrival of the dessert, breaking the tension. We made conversation while we indulged in macarons with whipped cream. The sparks between us were now on a low simmer, though I had a hunch it was only because Carter was keeping his hands to himself.

"You know, I'm going to try and sniff samples with the lights turned off. I think it's going to be an interesting experiment."

"You always look for ways to improve processes?"

"Of course. How else can I stay on top of things? But in this case, I don't know if it will improve the process. I just think it might provide an alternative perspective. I like trying out new things."

Once we finished the food, Carter asked, "Do you want to drink anything else?"

He'd put his hand on my lower back, slipping his thumb under my blouse, and my skin sizzled at the contact. And just like that, those sparks turned from simmering to explosive.

"We can go," I whispered. How could he set me on edge with such an innocent touch? Or maybe it was the cumulative effect of all the times he'd touched me before. I'd barely got the words out when he asked for the bill. Someone was impatient.

***
Carter

I made a concerted effort to keep my hands off Val on the way home. Once inside, she looked over her shoulder and asked, "Do I have you all night?"

"Yes, you do. The girls' nanny is spending the night with them."

"She's been their nanny for a while?"

"Two years. But she's starting her master's next fall, so I'm going to have to look for someone else. She's Zachary's cousin."

"He's the partner in Sloane & Partners?"

"One of them, yes. Anthony is the other. I went to law school with them."

"Were they brainiacs like you?"

"Someone looked me up."

She gave me a cute smile as we moved through the semidark living room. We weren't making much progress because I was keeping her flush against me, kissing her neck and shoulders, occasionally her lips too.

"I did it after you looked me up. You finished college earlier than anyone else. While working odd jobs, right?"

"What can I say? I never needed more sleep than five hours a night."

"I'm grouchy if I don't get eight."

"Noted."

"Also, I'm grouchy if you make noise in the

morning."

"Also noted. I drove my roommates at Harvard insane with my sleep schedule."

She chuckled. "I can imagine. You went there for law school, right?"

"Yes. Got my undergraduate degree from UCLA and went to Harvard for law school."

"You know, we could have met at Harvard. Landon and I had scholarships, but we gave them up when we had to come back to LA to look after the little ones."

"I didn't know that."

"It all worked out, but we had to be... flexible, you know?"

"Yeah, I do. It's why I decided to open up my own law firm. I wanted to call the shots."

"You're hot when you call the shots. What made you come back to LA after you finished law school?"

"Got the best job offer here, and I like the city."

I felt her smile against my cheek just as we reached the staircase, and I kissed her against the banister. I was so starved for this woman that I knew we wouldn't make it to the bedroom. Val parted her lips instantly for me, driving me crazy. My hands were on her waist, and she pressed her elbows lightly over my fingers, as if telling me not to let go. As if. I was beginning to think I wouldn't ever be able to let go.

I'd gone for so long without affection aside

from my family that I honestly had gotten good at ignoring that bone-deep loneliness. But now that Val was in my life, I felt that absence like a physical emptiness that ached. And I knew that only Val could fill it.

But she had a rough few years behind her. She deserved an uncomplicated relationship, one where the other person didn't have as much baggage and responsibilities as I did.

She gasped when I bit lightly at her shoulder.

"I've been dreaming about touching you like this for days," I murmured. I found the zipper of her skirt and lowered it. Then I pushed the fabric down, and the skirt pooled at her feet. She was wearing a thong that only covered the essential parts, and I sucked in a breath.

"Fuck, you're too beautiful."

I palmed each ass cheek, kneading it, and then I lowered myself, pushing down her panties slowly, then drawing my tongue even slower over the parts it had covered. Pleasure shot through me. She gasped, doubling over.

"Sit on the staircase," I said. "We won't make it upstairs. I want to taste you now."

She moved backward as if she felt the intensity of my desire like a physical force. Her legs wobbled. She sat on a stair, leaning with her elbows on the one above. I spread her thighs wide and kissed her right inner thigh, then swiped my hands under her ass, lifting her up slightly. I wanted easier access. She must have realized it because a tremor shook her. I was so turned on, it was almost painful. My thumbs reached up to her entrance, and I parted her wide.

"Carter." Her breath came out in a rush when I brought my mouth down on her. I planned to overwhelm her with pleasure, working her up, sucking and stroking where she needed it most.

Her climax was so swift and powerful that she cried out, closing her thighs, almost trapping me between them. My breath was ragged as I lowered her ass again and kissed the tops of her thighs.

She licked her lips as I helped her up. Turning around, she led me up the stairs.

"Hey! No more of that until we reach the bedroom." She pushed my hand away when I touched her ass.

"Why, you afraid we'll only make it to the top of the staircase?"

"You know it."

Chapter Nineteen
Val

Smelling samples was one of the finest pleasures in life, as far as I was concerned. Currently, I'd smeared three fragrances on my left forearm and three on the right one.

My fellow chemists were up in arms about this, first because the skin's chemistry altered the smell, and second because after sniffing three fragrances, the nose became too overwhelmed to tell the finer differences.

That was the theory. In practice, I knew that most people headed to a store and tried as many fragrances as possible, even on their skin. No one had time to try only three, then go back another time for more.

In any case, I'd identified most of our iconic fragrances by breaking the rules, so I planned to keep doing it.

I was alone in the small room because I asked not to be disturbed when I was sampling. I needed to concentrate—pick up on the finer notes, try to imagine what sort of emotion or reaction they could bring out in a customer. Sometimes I even wrote marketing briefings while I was at it. The conversation with Davis two weeks ago was at the back of my mind. I was semiconsciously wondering what kind of fragrances we could make for the potential exclusive line. Shaking my head, I resolved to concentrate on the task at hand before I went back to my office to compose an email to our sales associates. It was the end of November, and the Christmas rush was almost upon us.

Midway through the process, I heard commotion in the corridor, even though the door was shut.

I listened carefully, frowning when two of my newest employees ooh-ed and aah-ed. Then another familiar voice spoke.

"Of course we can take pictures, ladies."

Jace was visiting. That was weird. I grew downright concerned when I heard Hailey's voice as well. Had something happened? Whenever we met during the week, we met elsewhere, because my office was far away from everything.

When both he and Hailey entered the room, I scrutinized them. They looked happy and relaxed, so I relaxed too.

"This is a surprise." A very welcome surprise. I might not like being interrupted while sniffing samples, but I made exceptions for my siblings.

"Thought we'd pay you a visit," Hailey said. "We also brought lunch."

She held up a takeout bag, and my stomach rumbled in anticipation.

"Let's go upstairs. I don't want the smell of

food lingering here. It'll make testing harder."

Up the stairs we went and into the smaller of the two break rooms. It was empty. Most employees went out for lunch, and those who didn't preferred the other one because it opened up onto a balcony.

My siblings had brought quinoa and avocado salad, and as we dug in, I studied them. This wasn't a random visit. Hailey held her shoulders slightly raised, which meant she was in work mode, not relaxing mode, and Jace glanced at her from time to time.

"So, full disclosure, we're not here just for lunch," Hailey said eventually. "I had an idea."

"I'm listening."

"You know that our brother here is rather famous."

I feigned having to think it over. "Really? I couldn't tell. I think two of my girls tripped over their own feet for a picture with you."

His fame was unusual, because soccer typically didn't get as much attention in the US as basketball or hockey.

But my brother was more famous for being attractive than for playing soccer. It all started a few years ago when he appeared in a high-profile commercial. The internet exploded.

Then GQ ran a list of sexiest soccer players, and his fame carried over from the internet to the real world. In a town full of stars, it was saying something that Jace was so popular.

"Three, actually." Jace flashed a sheepish

smile.

"And I know you need a model for your fragrance line for men," Hailey continued.

"Yes," I said slowly.

"She wants to offer me up as tribute," Jace said with a wink. "Now that I'm famous and all that. She didn't even give me the time of day before."

"Don't egg me on before I've even finished my lunch. It's a dangerous endeavor," Hailey warned.

"Wow." I looked directly at Jace. "You're interested in that? You never told me."

"You never asked. I thought maybe you were looking for something else."

I cocked a brow. "Tall, handsome, and voted sexiest soccer star second year in a row? You're hot property, brother. I'd love to if you're game for it."

"I am."

Hailey clapped her hands. "I knew this would work out."

I looked between them, trying to put two and two together.

"How did you end up discussing this? Did you meet during Hailey's office hours to talk about marketing opportunities? Don't you specialize in PR scandals, sister?"

"She always catches on," Jace murmured in a defeated tone.

Hailey sighed. "He needed my advice for another matter, but we ended up discussing this as well."

Alarm bells were ringing in my mind. If he

needed Hailey's expertise, shit had hit the fan.

"Jace… what happened?"

My brother hesitated, then said, "Someone wrote to the club, insisting she's pregnant with my kid, and that if they didn't give out my contact info she'd go to the press."

I went still as a statue.

"Is it true?" I asked eventually.

Jace dipped his chin to his chest. "Low blow, sister. Thought you'd be on my side instantly."

"I'm always on your side," I clarified. "I just want to know the facts."

"No, of course it's not true. I've never even met the woman. The club's PR department usually deals with this without even telling us. Apparently people will invent all sorts of things to get our personal information."

"I don't understand. Why is this an issue, then?"

"She gave a very detailed account of what I did while I was out at a pub to celebrate a victory. It seemed real, and it gave our PR people pause. Which is when I turned to our dearest sister for advice."

"The Lords' PR people and I reviewed the footage of all the security cameras at the pub. We'd found out what she looked like by searching her name on Facebook," Hailey said. "She'd been at the pub that night, watching him, which was why she could give all those details. But they never even spoke, and she left before he did."

I remembered them whispering together

during the past two Friday dinners. I'd ask why they hadn't shared this with all of us like I'd told them about my issues with Beauty SkinEssence, but I knew Hailey's modus operandi: she only shared a problem after she'd solved it. I hadn't known that Jace also subscribed to that.

"It took some time to get the footage and look through it, but when she was confronted with the evidence, she dropped the issue," Hailey explained. "Then Jace and I moved on to happier topics, which included him stripping for your ads."

Jace groaned. "I only agreed to think about shirtless ads."

"We'll wear him down," my sister fake whispered to me.

"We'll do whatever you're comfortable with," I assured Jace.

"But you'll persuade me to be comfortable with stripping?" he guessed.

I grinned. "I promise not to."

"Well, you're no fun today." Hailey pouted, then checked the time on her phone. "I have to go already." She stood up, kissing us both on the cheeks. Jace didn't make a move to leave.

"We drove here separately," he offered at my questioning glance.

"Are you okay?" I asked him after Hailey left.

"Yes. I just didn't need this drama, but I guess no one ever needs it."

Jace was a happy-go-lucky kind of person. He'd always been that way, as if nothing could faze or bother him. But lately, I'd sensed that something was off with him. I hadn't voiced that thought because I was trying to be less of a mother hen to them all, but I didn't want to stay silent anymore.

"There's more bothering you," I said slowly.

"When I decided to play professional soccer, I wanted to do it because I loved the game. But lately it feels like the game is on the back burner. Ever since the GQ title, things became insane. I can't complain, fame brought me many advantages too, and I've enjoyed them, it's just that...."

"What?"

"It's a bit too much. The pressure, the expectations. All these people coming out of the woodwork wanting to befriend me. I envy you. You built all this, but you're in the shadows."

"Are you sure you want to go on with the advertising gig? It won't help the cause."

"I think it's time I got used to all of this, took advantage of it. Listen to me, rambling on about first world problems." He shook his head.

"Hey, problems are problems. And grappling with change is natural, I think. It's a process, like everything else."

"What if I'm just not cut out for it?" he said in a slightly lower tone, and I could tell it was weighing on him.

Usually, when I gave advice or reassurance, I tried to put myself in the shoes of the other person, but in this case, I was out of my depth. My brand was built around the products, not myself, so I'd always been in the shadows.

"Jace, you're the Lords' most valuable player. Your game is excellent. That's the important thing. The rest is secondary, but if it's becoming too much, I'm sure you can take measures to avoid the limelight."

"I know, but it also seems stupid not to capitalize on my luck. I know that this career isn't forever. If I'm unlucky, an injury can take me out at any time. All these contracts for commercials are good money that I'll need later. In Dad's words, I just need to toughen up. This won't last forever anyway. I have maybe ten years left to play, and then everyone will forget who I am. Sorry for laying all this on you. I guess I just needed to vent."

"You have nothing to be sorry for. You can always talk to me."

"Thanks, sis. How is it going with Beauty SkinEssence?"

"It feels like we're playing ping-pong. Their lawyer makes a move, then mine, then theirs again. Lawyer fees are piling up. I don't even want to think about it. Sooo, since you're here…."

"Oh, no. I know what you're going to ask."
"How?"

"You were in the sampling room. And you want to drag me there with you."

"A man's perspective always helps."

Jace grinned. I grinned back.

"Fine, I'll come with you. But only because I feel guilty for dumping all this on you."

"Awww. I love you too."

Chapter Twenty
Val

I tortured my brother for about an hour before calling it a day. I wasn't trying to be a nuisance, but it required hard work to get more out of Jace than "This is okay" and "This is okay too." I needed the nitty-gritty. If he were part of a focus group, he'd be a tough cookie to crack.

"Do you have time to grab a tea?" I asked as we made our way to the break room. "Leta just texted me that she's in the area and dropping by."

Leta was a good friend of mine. I'd met her a few years ago at a conference, and we hit it right off.

"Sure."

I narrowed my eyes at Jace. He looked a little too excited. I pinched his arm.

"Leta is my friend. Don't go after her and make things weird."

"Are you implying I'd break her heart? You have no faith in me."

"You're right. When it comes to this, I have zero faith." I squinted. "Unless you're telling me you want to settle down?"

Jace looked shocked. "Sisters. Always up for stabbing you in the back."

"Never." I patted his cheek. There was a time when he'd relished all the media attention and the never-ending flings. But now it seemed he was ready to make some changes.

"You haven't answered my question, so I'll take it as a yes."

"Val," he said warningly.

"Come on, give me some details. Describe to me your ideal woman."

He squinted. "Please tell me you're not going to try and set me up."

"Are you crazy? That's what we have Pippa for. She knows her stuff. This is purely sisterly curiosity." And maybe fishing for information to pass on to Pippa. Maybe.

Our cousin, Pippa Bennett-Callahan was an excellent matchmaker, and even though she lived in San Francisco, I wouldn't put it past her to work her magic on Jace whenever she was visiting.

Leta was waiting for us in the doorway of the break room. She waved at me and smiled brightly at Jace. Oh boy. My brother's charm was hard at work, as usual. The thing was, he didn't even have to put any effort into it. That smile of his had been a heartbreaker since he'd turned thirteen. The rest of his appearance wasn't helping either. And neither was his fame.

Since the break room was already crowded, we took three mugs and headed into my office. I had a kettle and tea selection in there as well.

The three of us talked for about half an hour

before Jace got a call from his coach, and then he had to leave for an impromptu team meeting.

"Girl, your brother gets hotter every year," Leta commented after Jace left. "And I've had a year-long dry spell. He's single, right?"

"Umm… yes."

Leta smiled saucily, and I could tell she was about to pepper me with some more questions, but we were interrupted by Carter.

"Anne didn't say you had company." He looked between Leta and me.

"She probably thought Leta left with Jace. Carter, this is my friend Leta. Leta, Carter moved to the area some time ago. We're practically neighbors. He's an excellent lawyer."

Carter looked at me expectantly, only casting his gaze away when Leta stretched out her hand. I noticed her blatant perusal of him, that saucy smile she was flashing him. I looked down into my cup, breathing in and out a few times. My stomach turned into a tight knot. Leta was a flirt, and she was beautiful. I looked up between my lashes, studying Carter's expression as he shook her hand. I detected politeness, then looked back at my cup. I was afraid to look too close and possibly discover something more.

"I could use a good lawyer," Leta commented. "Do you have a business card?"

"Not on me, but Val can pass on my contact information."

"Excellent. I'd love to pick your brain. We

should grab dinner sometime. On me, of course."

My heart was now lodged in my throat. Despite myself, I glanced up. Leta wasn't looking at Carter as if she wanted to pick his brain. She was looking at him as if she wanted to take off his clothes. What the hell? She'd been all flirty with Jace, and now she was making a move on Carter?

And speaking of Carter, his gaze was on me. His expression was hard. Intense. An awkward moment followed, in which Leta looked at Carter, clearly expecting an answer, but he kept his eyes trained on me.

Eventually, Leta said, "I need to freshen up my makeup before I go. The bathroom is third down the hall, right?"

"Yes."

After Leta exited the room, I headed to the small table against the wall where I kept the tea.

"Do you want tea? I just bought a delicious herbal mix."

"No, I can't stay long. I just wanted to drop by and see you."

"Oh!" I felt all fuzzy inside.

"Yeah."

There was a slight tightness in his voice I didn't like.

"Carter, is something wrong? You're acting strange."

I poured more hot water into my cup. I hadn't even heard Carter move through the room, but now I felt him right behind me. He rested his hands on either side of my hips. He hadn't answered me, I realized, which meant something was wrong. My heart began to race as we stood completely still. I felt his hot breath tickling my skin.

"You introduced me to Leta as a lawyer and neighbor. As just a neighbor."

"Oh. I didn't realize—"

When he spoke next, his lips were on the back of my neck. He was whispering in that low, seductive voice that turned my knees weak.

"I've kissed every inch of you. I can make you come in so many ways. Maybe I should remind you of all the ways in which I'm not just a neighbor."

He moved his hand from my hip around to my front.

He was only touching my stomach in small circles, but that motion was the one he used to caress me intimately when I was nearing the edge. I sucked in a breath. I couldn't believe I was so turned on.

"Did you tell your family about me, Valentina?"

"I told my sisters and Landon. Haven't mentioned it to Will and Jace yet because they tend to be a little overprotective."

"But you'll tell them?"

"Yes."

He whirled me around until we were facing each other, then he cupped my face. I was startled by that intense look in his gaze, the hard lines on his face, the tightness in his jaw.

"Are you sure?"

"I'm sure."

His eyes were searching me as if he was trying to read every thought and every emotion. I tore my gaze from him, focusing instead on his shoulder. I hoped he couldn't sense my inner turmoil. Everything was overwhelming even for me: my hope that this could turn into more than a fling battling with my fear of having my heart crushed again.

He wanted my family to know, and yet he still hadn't asked me to spend any time with him and the girls. It had been about a month since we'd started sleeping together. I'd said he was a neighbor because I didn't know how else to introduce him. I didn't want to put a label on this that he wasn't comfortable with.

I couldn't put my predicament into words, and when he brought his mouth to my neck, raining kisses from the base right up to that sensitive spot below my ear, I couldn't even think.

"Jesus, Carter!"

"I love hearing you say my name."

Pulling back, he drew his thumb over my lips, and I parted them, darting the tip of my tongue forward. He swallowed hard, locking his gaze on my mouth. He hadn't expected this. Then he took me by surprise, pinning me with his hips against the edge of the table. He took one of my hands in his, then slid his own down to clasp it around my wrist, two fingers pressing on my pulse point before he lowered his head and planted an openmouthed kiss where he'd touched before. God, I was so aroused....

He brought his mouth closer, speaking against my lips. "Are you turned on?"

I was aware that I was breathing faster. My entire body was on edge. But still, I shook my head playfully. Carter cocked a brow. I looked between us as I felt his hand slide further up under my blouse, cupping one breast. Then he pulled it out and moved both hands on my waist. A cocky smile played on his lips.

"What are you doing?" I whispered.

"Giving you a taste of what will come later tonight."

"Oh, yeah, what's that?"

"I'll leave you guessing."

"I think I have a few ideas."

"Of course you do. You're a wicked little thing under your pencil skirts and blouses."

I jutted out my lower lip. "Are you calling me easy?"

"No, babe. I'm just calling you sexy."

"Are you trying to convince me to do sexy things with you in my office?"

"Maybe. Are you relenting?"

"Never." I tried to push him away before he got any other outrageous ideas, but the man wouldn't budge. "What if someone had seen us?" I pointed to the open door. Carter laughed, but his eyes were dark and glittering. I swatted his shoulder. "I mean it."

"Keep going like this and I'll lock the door and make you come against it."

Holy shit. I could tell that he meant every

word. Part of me wanted to keep egging him on so he'd make good on his promise, but... damn. I was in my office. And Leta would be back any second now.

Speak of the devil.... Carter finally stepped to one side when we heard footsteps approaching.

I wasn't aware of how possessive his grip on me looked until I saw Leta's brows climb into her hairline as she took both of us in. We were leaning against the goodies table, side by side. Carter had slung an arm around my lower back, and his hand was resting on my hipbone.

"Val," she said coyly. "You didn't tell me you two were a couple."

Out of the corner of my eye, I saw Carter smile. He didn't move his hand one inch as he replied, "We are."

Chapter Twenty-One
Carter

"Orange juice is coming right up," I called out to Peyton and April. A cold had hit both of them two days ago. They were feeling better but weren't one hundred percent healthy yet, so I'd announced at the office that I'd work from home today as well. While I waited for the juicer to fill the cup, I downed my second cup of coffee. I didn't much feel like a lawyer today; more like the walking dead. I'd been up with Peyton all night. She barely slept whenever she was sick, and I'd taken to sleeping on the small couch in her room on those nights. Sometimes she climbed next to me, nestling her little body against me, asking for stories because they kept the monsters from coming out from under the bed.

I'd set them up in the living room, because April had proclaimed she didn't want to be stuck in her room during the daytime too, and Peyton was still at the age where she did everything her sister said. They were both asleep as I brought them orange juice. April's favorite Netflix show was still playing on her laptop, which was in a precarious position in her lap. I removed it, careful not to wake them up. They needed sleep. I did too, but a million work emails stood between me and sleep.

My apartment was a mix of ultramodern and classic, but the girls' touch was visible everywhere. They were messy, but I liked it. My office was the only orderly area. I sat behind my desk, drafting documents for three cases simultaneously. Around noon, the girls woke up, and we ordered in. As we finished, I knew I had to call Val. I'd postponed this for as long as possible, but I couldn't leave the girls with the nanny this evening. I didn't like to leave them when they weren't feeling well.

I'd had plans with Val, and I'd really wanted to see her. I moved into another room to make the call.

"Hey," I greeted when she picked up.

"Hey."

"So listen, I know we had plans this evening, and I'm very sorry to cancel them. I can't leave my apartment today."

"What happened?"

"The girls have a cold, and I'm working from home."

"Oh, I'm so sorry."

"They're better now, but I don't want to leave them."

"I understand, of course." After a pause, she added, "I can stop by, if you want."

I hadn't expected that.

"I'd love that."

"Do you need anything?"

"No, we're good. I'll order dinner in."

"I can cook something."

"You don't have to do that."

"But I'm a great chef."

"Humble too."

"Never when it comes to my cooking."

"Don't worry, we don't need anything."

"Okay if I drop by at seven thirty?"

"Sure."

It was only after hanging up that I wondered if this was such a great idea. Until now, our encounters had always been light and playful, and I'd kept what I had with Val separate from everything else. Those moments had been in a bubble of their own. What if reality would burst our bubble?

The truth was, I wanted to see Val too much to worry about anything else. We hadn't spent Thanksgiving together last week, because I flew with the girls to visit my parents.

She arrived at seven thirty on the dot. Peyton was waiting by the front door. She was beside herself with excitement every time she was about to meet someone new, but then when she came face-to-face with said person, she hid.

Predictably, the second I opened the door, Peyton stepped behind my legs.

Val grinned at me before crouching to her level.

"Hi, Peyton. I'm Valentina. You can call me Val. All my friends do."

Peyton tentatively tilted her head to one side, but when Val held out her arms, she stepped out.

"I'm your friend?" she asked suspiciously.

"If you want to be. I would love to be your friend."

Peyton inched closer, then threw herself in Val's open arms, kissing her cheek. It was sloppy and wet, but Val didn't seem to mind. Warmth spread in my chest as I watched the two of them.

Val had cheated. She'd brought the girls sweets, and both April and Peyton munched on them happily.

"Val, you're my hero," April exclaimed. "Carter, take notes."

I scowled at my niece. When April was out of earshot, I turned to Val. "Sweets?"

"Comfort food." She shrugged as if it was the most natural thing in the world.

"I usually make them something healthy when they have a cold."

Val looked as if she was fighting a smile, then whispered, "Tell you a secret. No one actually wants healthy food when they're out of sorts. It just drives home the fact that you're feeling like crap. Not the best mood lifter, if you ask me."

"Interesting logic."

She grinned. "It might be a little... different, but hey, worse than being ill is being sick and grumpy. And grumpiness was just as contagious in the Connor household as a cold. So I cheated and twisted rules to the max to keep that from happening. But hey, everyone grew up to be healthy and responsible adults, so I'm not feeling too guilty."

She was lovely. I leaned in to kiss her, intending only to give her a quick peck, but at the first taste of her mouth I became hungry for more. I wanted to lose myself in this woman, explore her for days. When she rewarded me with a small moan, I became even greedier. But I couldn't touch her right now, so I took a step back.

"You make me lose my head, woman."

"Hmmm... I wonder why that is."

"Could be your soft skin." I kissed her shoulder. "Or this gorgeous ass." I squeezed it once before moving my hand slowly around the front. "Or your tight, delicious—"

"Carter." She almost hissed my name. I grinned. "You can't say things like these when there are kids around."

"They can't hear us. And I can't help myself around you."

"You say that as if I'm some sex goddess."

"You are."

She narrowed her eyes, tapping her fingers against her cheek. "I can't tell if you mean it or you're buttering me up for something."

"I never say things I don't mean. But that doesn't mean I'm not buttering you up." My voice was solemn, but I was laughing with her as we joined the girls in the living room. I suggested a movie, but April wasn't in the mood for watching anything.

"I've sat around all day watching things. I'm bored," April said.

Val bit her lower lip. "What would you like to

do?"

"I don't know. Hey, where did you buy that belt? It's cool."

"One of my favorite online shops. I'll show it to you." After a moment, she added, "Do you like closet parties?"

April piped up. "I don't know what it is, but it has two of my favorite words in it, so I'm game."

"We take a look at your clothes and how we can mix and match them to get different outfits than what you usually wear."

April looked excited for the first time in twelve hours. Peyton was hanging around my neck like a little monkey, looking excitedly from her sister to Val.

"That sounds awesome."

"And very scary to me," I added, just to play devil's advocate.

Val moved closer to April, whispering loud enough for me to hear, "Should we punish him for that by insisting he join us?"

"Nah, he'll just ruin our buzz. Besides, I'm dying for some girl time."

My heart gave a little squeeze at their playful banter. And then I decided to surprise them.

"You know what? I'll join you."

Val winked. April grimaced.

"Fine, but you must promise not to give your opinion… unless it's a positive one," April said.

"I love your idea of democracy. I'll take my laptop with me. Need to finalize a few things."

April led the way to her room. Peyton, never one to miss any excitement, ran along next to her. Val walked a few feet behind them. I had a perfect view of that gorgeous ass of hers. Damn, the way she moved, that sensual sway of her hips, was making my mouth water. Was she doing it on purpose, to set me on edge?

When she cast a saucy smile over her shoulder, I had my answer. As payback, I slid closer to her and pinched her ass.

Val didn't quite manage to muffle her sound of surprise, which caught April's attention. When she turned around, I immediately schooled my expression. I felt as if our roles were reversed and I was the teenager trying to get away with fondling the girl he liked.

As April and Val took out most of the clothes in the dresser, spreading them on the bed, I sat at April's desk, trying to get some more work done, but I couldn't concentrate. The girls were taking this seriously. Even Peyton was hanging on to every word Val said.

"How do you even get these ideas? I wouldn't have paired those, but they look fabulous," April exclaimed.

"I took a personal course with a fashion consultant once."

"You're officially the coolest person I know."

Val laughed. "I don't know about that. But I'd just started my business, and since I wasn't tied to a dress code like in my old job, I knew I was liable to go crazy. My sense of fashion has always been a little weird, but there is a fine line between different and ridiculous."

"Well, I think you're a knockout."

Sometime during this exchange, my heartbeat had become erratic. They were having fun, I realized. Val wasn't patronizing the girls or finding them an inconvenience. This was so far off my past experiences that I hadn't even come to expect it any longer. It was partly why I liked to separate these sides of my personal life.

When April pulled her hair in a ponytail, trying out an outfit Val had come up with, I had déjà vu.

"You look just like Hannah," I told her. I missed my sister so much that some days it felt like a physical ache.

"I do, don't I?" April grinned before explaining to Val, "In all her pics, Mom looks like a runway model. She was definitely a fashionista."

"Am I a fashionista?" Peyton asked, frowning at the mirror as if searching for signs.

I laughed, but Val replied smoothly, "You're on your way to becoming one."

When April went to bring her favorite scarf from the foyer, with Peyton trailing after her, I kept my eyes trained on Val. She caught me looking and blushed, but I didn't take my eyes off her. Even though I was sitting in the opposite corner of the room, the sexual tension filling the air was palpable. Eventually Val focused on rearranging some outfits on the bed. I loved it when she wouldn't even look at me because she was afraid that if she did, she wouldn't be able to resist me.

I left the room shortly after the girls returned, partly because I couldn't stand being so close to Val and not touching her or imagining how our life would look if she was permanently part of it, and partly because the activity was too girly for me. By the time I finished drafting the third document, it was ten o'clock. I pressed the heels of my palms against my eyes, which had started to hurt. I'd just opened up a document with some statutes I wanted to brush up on when Val joined me in my home office.

She came next to me and leaned against the desk.

"How are the girls?"

"They fell asleep in April's bed. We had so much fun. April has great taste in fashion. And we discovered we have the same shoe size, which means I might lend her shoes at some point."

I glared at her.

"What?"

"Every pair of shoes I've seen on you is inappropriate."

"What? You loved them."

"On you. Not my teenage niece."

"Double standard much?"

I let out a low growl. Val grinned.

"You know what, you had me all convinced that you're this laid-back uncle... but you're not. I'm going to switch teams. The other team needs me more."

"I see."

"I love that you keep their parents' memory alive," she said unexpectedly.

"I don't want the girls to forget them, Peyton especially. She was a baby when they passed away, and I think that mentioning little facts now and then makes the girls feel as if they knew their mom and dad without making them sad. They miss them."

"And you miss your sister."

"I do. In the beginning it was honestly a little painful to look at April, because she looks so much like Hannah. I hope my sister is happy with the way I'm raising her girls."

"I have no doubt that she is." She watched me with warm eyes. "How did it happen?"

"They went skiing and were caught in an avalanche. It was an excruciating time, especially while the search went on. We were all hoping they'd make it out, and then…. It was tough."

"I can imagine."

"I have no idea how I kept it together."

"You're a strong man, Carter."

"My parents were devastated. Especially Dad."

"How is he? I think you mentioned he had hip surgery."

"Just spoke to Mom today. His recovery is slow. It's a good thing she's there with him, even though the girls miss her."

Val glanced at my laptop. "Are you done with that?"

In response, I shut it off, then immediately pulled Val into my lap.

"Thanks for coming here today."

"My pleasure. Though I think I've given April shopping ideas that are dangerous for your credit card. Maybe I should have warned you before that I'm known for giving dangerous shopping ideas. My sisters keep telling me so."

"They do?"

"Oh, yeah. I gave them the shopping bug when we were kids. It was mostly at thrift stores, but people seriously underestimate those. You can find gems. I even had a sewing machine for repairs or alterations. Spent many evenings on it after I returned from the pub."

"That sounds like your days were long."

"They were."

"Did you ever feel like you were failing?"

"Very often."

That surprised me. "I feel like that almost every week."

Val placed a kiss on my jaw, then went on to my neck, which made it hard to think.

"I have an outsider's point of view, and I can tell you that you're not."

"But you might be biased because you like me so much."

She straightened up, looking me straight in the eyes. "Nope, I'm one hundred percent objective."

"So you sewed after you returned from the pub, huh? And you also planned your business?"

"Well, I didn't do it at the same time. I only started planning once everyone was old enough to sew their own clothes without losing any fingers."

"Free time wasn't a thing for you back then, I take it?"

She laughed. "You could say that. By the time I opened the business though, everyone was older. They didn't need me so much and I didn't even know what to do with so much free time. So I basically did the jobs of three people for years."

"I know what you mean. You condition and train yourself for so long that it's the only thing you know. It becomes your normal."

"Exactly. Everyone was telling me I had to slow down, but I was like, what are you talking about? This is slowing down. I'm doing better now, though. I have a healthy balance, and I enjoy my chill life and my time off."

I stilled, hoping that my less than "chill" life wouldn't scare her away, because I needed this woman in my life. Val and I had been dealt similar life blows, only we were at different stages. She had those busy years behind her and was enjoying her freedom, while I would still be in the thick of it for the next ten years.

I traced kisses along her jawline, then down the column of her throat. She shuddered, and I moved my lips over her collarbone, up to her shoulder, pushing off one strap.

"What should I do about this dress? It covers far too much."

"Take it off?"

I smiled against her skin, finding the hem and lifting it up to her knees, which were propped at my sides, then further up her thighs until her legs were completely on display.

But then Peyton's voice sounded throughout the apartment, calling me.

I took in a deep breath, trying to compose myself. "I'm going to move Peyton to her room. It might take a while for her to fall asleep. Do you want to spend the night here?"

The muscles around my middle clenched. I hadn't planned on asking her this yet. I'd figured I would ease her in, take things one step at a time. But now every fiber of my being was strummed tight, waiting for her answer.

"Are you sure?"

"If you'd rather not—"

"I want to."

I looked her straight in the eyes, trying to gauge what this meant for her. Was she staying because I could show her a good time in bed, or was she feeling this connection between us grow deeper too? Did she want to let it grow and deepen? Or was she content with the way things were?

Peyton called for me again, interrupting the moment. I kissed Val's forehead. "Come on. I'll show you where you can shower."

Chapter Twenty-Two
Val

I took my sweet time showering, and when I came out I heard Carter talking on the phone in his office. It hadn't taken long to get Peyton to bed after all. That little girl reminded me so much of Hailey. So curious and sweet, though Hailey had never been shy.

I shimmied my hips to an imaginary song in Carter's bedroom, half listening to check if he was still talking so I'd know when to storm in and steal the show. When I'd passed his office, I'd heard the words deposition and witness, so I gathered it was a work conversation. It wouldn't do to tempt him while he was at it, no matter how much I was dying to do just that.

When I couldn't hear him talking anymore, I tightened the robe around me and tiptoed down the corridor before remembering the girls' bedrooms were on the other side of the apartment.

As I stepped into his office, his leather chair was turned toward the window, but I knew he was sitting there. His presence filled the room. I intended to surprise him, but he must have heard me, because he spun around with his chair. Even in the semidarkness, I saw his smile.

"Sorry this took so long. I thought you'd fall asleep by now."

"Nope."

"Close the door behind you, Val. Lock it."

I swallowed, the rich baritone of his voice sending tingles of anticipation down my spine. The second he heard the key turn, he added another command. "Come here."

When I stopped in front of him, he straightened in his chair, bringing one hand to the side of my knee, skimming it up my outer thigh.

"Tell me what you're wearing under the robe."

"Nothing."

"Good answer."

He tugged at the robe until it opened. He kissed the underside of one breast. When he sucked the nipple into his mouth, I clenched my thighs reflexively. Carter rose from the leather chair, capturing my mouth, kissing me deeply. He cupped the back of my head, tilting it at the angle he wanted, taking control of the kiss. It was wild, needy kissing. My knees weakened with every stroke of his tongue.

"You came here to tempt me?" he spoke against my lips.

"Absolutely. I plan to unleash all my seduction skills to lure you into bed."

"I want to fuck you right here in this office, Valentina. I want to make memories with you inside here, so when I'm by myself, I can remember how it was to have you spread wide on my desk, to sink inside you."

I became slick just from his words. As if suspecting this, he drew his middle finger across my opening, making me whimper.

"You're so responsive."

He took off the robe, pushing the leather chair out of the way, then led me by the hand until I was standing right in front of his desk. He was behind me, kissing the back of my neck and my shoulder blades before raining kisses down my back.

"Lean forward and spread your legs wide for me."

I leaned on my elbows, parting my legs. Carter stopped touching me altogether for a few seconds, but before I could have time to miss his warmth, his mouth was on my slick center, his tongue darting in and out of me. I could barely take the sudden assault on my senses, and when Carter pressed two fingers to my clit, my thighs shook.

I couldn't hold myself on my elbows any longer, so I leaned all the way forward until my breasts were pressing against the cold table. My hands were itching to grab or pull, so I stretched my arms forward until I reached the edge of the desk. I gripped it hard, pressing myself against his mouth.

An orgasm slammed into me, spurred by his mouth and his fingers. It took a long time to ride out the wave of pleasure, and when I straightened up, I swayed a little.

Carter held his arms around me, resting his nose in the crook of my neck. His breath was coming out in short, hot bursts. His erection pressed against my ass. We weren't nearly done for tonight. I wiggled my ass a little, luring a groan out of him before I turned around.

He smiled before kissing me, and then I heard the sound of a belt being unbuckled and knew he couldn't stand not being inside me for one more minute. I pulled at the zipper, then pushed his pants down his legs. He lowered his boxers too before kicking both away. After taking off his shirt, he dropped onto the leather chair.

"Ride me."

Heart pounding, I approached him but didn't climb on top. I had plans first, so I lowered myself on my haunches between his thighs.

"What are you doing?"

"Giving you something to remember."

I wanted him to think about this every time he sat in this chair. I ran my palm from the velvety tip down to cup his balls, tugging a little as I took him in my mouth.

"Val!"

I bobbed my head up and down, bracing an arm on his thigh for support. He groaned my name again and again, but he didn't let me go to town for as long as I wanted.

"I want to be inside you."

He lifted me up, helping me climb on top of him. The chair was wide enough that I could comfortably rest my calves next to his thighs. I lowered myself on him inch by inch. He pushed his head back, pinching his eyes closed. I moved my lower body in a lazy rhythm. I loved being on top of him. I could touch and kiss him wherever I wanted: his biceps, his shoulders, his neck. I loved kissing his neck. The skin on his arms turned to goose bumps when I bit his Adam's apple lightly.

"Give me your mouth," he commanded. I continued to torment the sensitive skin on his neck. But then he took over, grabbing my ass with both hands and pulling me up and down on him. "Val, kiss me."

I straightened, and he captured my mouth, tangling our tongues. We were both moving. He was thrusting from below, and I slid my hips at a frantic pace. When he brought one hand between us, circling my clit, my insides strummed so tight that I felt I was going to split in two.

"Harder, please," I whispered.

He was pounding into me with more ferocity than before, but I wanted every last drop of passion. I didn't know how to put it in words, but my body did all the talking for me. I clawed at his shoulders, at his back, moving as fast as I could. As if feeling I needed more, he lifted me up, and my ass was on the wooden surface next.

Carter hooked an arm under each knee, pulling me right at the edge of the desk. When he drove inside me, pleasure swamped me like rings of fire, getting nearer and nearer to my center. He had unrestricted access to my clit, and he was using that advantage. Oh, how he was using it.

His thumb was barely caressing it, but it was driving me wild. "This is… oh fuck."

"That's it, Val. I want to feel you come. I want to hear you."

I didn't know if it was the pressure on my clit or his dirty words that did me in, but I clenched tight, holding on to his shoulders. Carter kept thrusting through my orgasm, until he cried out his own release, buckling over me, slamming his hands on the desk for support at either side of my arms. He groaned my name, driving into me until he was spent. Resting his head on my chest, he took in long, deep breaths and only pulled out a few minutes later, helping me stand. My legs were a little wobbly. If his shit-eating grin was anything to go by, he hadn't missed it.

He rested a hand possessively on my back. "I'm never going to be able to get any work done in here again."

I shrugged a shoulder playfully, and he pinched my ass. "That was my master plan all along."

Chapter Twenty-Three
Val

"Chop, chop. Come on, no slacking. The others are going to be here any minute now," I instructed one week later as I was preparing for Friday dinner. Jace and Hailey had arrived earlier, and I had roped them into helping me cook. Usually I didn't want more than one chef in the kitchen (unless it was a bare-chested, singing Carter; I'd eat burned toast just to have that view), but I was trying out a new dish today, and it turned out to be more complex than I'd thought.

"Hey, I'm working hard," Jace complained. "I'm just not good at it."

Hailey wasn't faring much better. She'd actually arrived earlier because she wanted to dish about her latest date, but with Jace around, that had to wait. But by the shimmy in my sister's movements, I gathered it had gone better than fine.

It had been a hectic week, in which I'd finally managed to try out the "sampling in the dark" technique, and I liked it so much that I was going to incorporate it into my routine from now on. Whenever I'd had a free moment, I'd been perusing my favorite online stores, and sent April so many links that she could renew her entire wardrobe. I'd told April to blame me for any outfits Carter might deem… inappropriate. I hoped Carter wouldn't have a panic attack when she showed him the selection.

"Considering you had two hopeless cases as kitchen aides, I'd say this turned out pretty well," Jace said a while later as he tasted the final product.

"Hey, don't sell yourself short," I replied after swallowing a spoonful. "This is great. Before you know it, you'll be a cook. A very attractive quality in a guy, I must say."

"Yeah, what's that, Jace? Val tells me you're on your way to settling down," Hailey teased.

"You already informed everyone in the family?"

"Of course."

Jace narrowed his eyes at me. "I thought you said you wouldn't meddle."

I widened my eyes mockingly. "Me? Never. But I told Hailey, and if she wants to interfere, I can't be held responsible, can I?"

"You don't have to worry about me, little bro. I'm not going to do anything." She'd started to make salad dressing.

"Awwww, sis. I'm knee deep in shit. You're using your 'PR' tone. The one that means I'm just going to pacify this poor schmuck but do what I want anyway."

Hailey stopped putting salt in the salad. "When did you become so perceptive?"

Jace winked. "A while ago. So, 'fess up."

"Well... you do have quite the fan club among my friends."

"You're not going to warn me off anyone, unlike our oldest sister here?"

"I have far more trust in you," Hailey said solemnly.

"That's my Hailey."

Once everyone had arrived and was seated at the table, I realized I had no herbs for the salad, so I went out in the yard to pick some fresh thyme and coriander. I was crouched, pulling at the herbs, when I heard the voice.

"Damn, that's a sight for sore eyes."

I straightened up and nearly lost my balance as I whirled around to face Carter.

My face split in a grin. "What are you doing here?"

"You said you were home, and I thought I'd surprise you."

He glanced at the herbs, then at the house as laughter filtered through the open windows.

"You've got company?"

"Yeah. My entire family is here. Friday night dinner, remember?"

I'd invited him twice, but he always had plans with the girls Friday evening, so I hadn't insisted. After he'd asked me to sleep at his house last week, I'd wanted to bring it up again, but hadn't had the chance. This was the perfect opportunity.

"I hadn't realized they're a regular thing."

"I've made them a regular thing ever since Will turned eighteen and moved out. I think the likelihood of an asteroid colliding with earth is higher than me canceling a Friday dinner."

Carter laughed as his gaze perused me lazily, igniting my body. I was certain he could do this a million times and it still would affect me.

"Do you want to join us?" I asked, though I was trying to mentally envision what would happen when I introduced him to my brothers. He must have mistaken my worry for reticence because he frowned.

"If you'd rather keep it family only, I understand."

"Of course not. I'd love to have you and the girls here, but I know you always have plans on Friday. Where are they now?"

"Playdate with a friend."

"Come on, let's head inside. But I'm warning you, it can be a bit crazy when we're all together, and my brothers can be a bit overprotective."

Carter gave me a sinful smile. "That's what brothers are for. I still need to talk to you about all those links you sent to April."

I assessed the glint in his eyes. It was somewhere between dangerous and delicious. I shimmied a little as we climbed the staircase up to the house. Carter placed an arm around my lower back, his palm pressing against the side of my waist. A spark of awareness traveled from where his fingertips touched all the way to my navel, and lower still.

Hmm… I should have stolen some kisses when I had the chance.

The moment we entered the dining room, everyone went quiet.

"Everyone, this is Carter." I gestured with one hand, still clutching the herbs in the other.

Carter shook hands with everybody, and I could see the wheels spinning in my brothers' minds. They'd known I was seeing Carter. I told them after he and I talked in my office, but they hadn't pried. Yet as I took in Will's and Jace's expressions, I was sure they were about to do a whole lot of prying. Landon looked calm, as always.

"I'll take care of the herbs," Hailey offered, and I gave her a thankful glance as I handed over the thyme and coriander. I didn't think leaving Carter to fend off Jace and Will when they were in protective mode was the best thing.

Will started the interrogation, of course. He might not wear a badge anymore, but he still put his detective skills to use. I glanced at Paige, his fiancée, who was watching him closely. I knew she'd have my back if Will came on too strong.

The atmosphere was friendly though. I wouldn't have to throttle either Jace or Will. Progress.

Midway through dinner, I was completely relaxed as we chitchatted about a particularly fun moment at Lori and Graham's wedding.

Then Milo piped up to tell Carter, "Dad asked

for my permission before he married Mom. If you want, you can ask my permission too."

I felt as if my face was on fire. My nephew meant well and was simply being adorable as usual, but I couldn't help glancing at Carter out of the corner of my eye. Kids liked to repeat what adults said, and I didn't want Carter to think I'd told my family I had any expectations. I didn't want to scare him away.

"I'll certainly keep that in mind," Carter answered jovially.

After dinner, we were playing badminton.

"Want to join us?" I asked Carter.

"Sure. The girls are spending the night at their friends' houses."

"You had great plans, huh?"

"You have no idea."

I grinned, unsuccessfully trying to ignore the way my body reacted to his words. This man was a walking danger for me. I'd planned to serve ice cream for dessert, but to my astonishment, I realized I didn't have enough.

"Change of plans," I told the room at large. "I'm going to buy a pie real quick."

There was a bakery nearby, and their pies were to die for. Before I left, I pulled Carter a little further away, whispering, "I'm sorry for the interrogation."

"It's all good. Nothing April's and Peyton's dates won't hear from me." He winked at me.

"Just ignore any sentence including the words

serious or future, okay?"

Carter didn't answer. He simply nodded, but his jaw seemed tight.

***

Carter

Once we headed out to Val's backyard, I went straight to the case with badminton rackets. When Will joined me, I didn't think anything of it. When Jace appeared on my other side, I suspected I was about to be cornered.

"Val told us you have two nieces," Jace said.

"April and Peyton. They're great girls. Both on their way to becoming troublemakers."

"Ah, we've had a few of those in our family."

"Hailey, right?"

"No, I· was the resident troublemaker," Jace corrected. "Though Hailey will try to claim that title for herself. Don't believe her."

Will cocked a brow. "I busted both of your asses and covered for you in equal measure."

Jace smirked. "Yeah, but you never knew which one was the bad influence, did you?"

I laughed, imagining Val putting up with all the Connors under one roof.

Jace turned to Will, hooking his thumb at him. "Don't let this one fool you with his ex-detective past. He was quite a troublemaker himself."

"I know. Val told me."

"She said that?" Will looked crestfallen.

"What else?"

I held up my hands in surrender. "Ask her. I can feel you guys turning against me just because I'm relaying the information. Don't shoot the messenger."

"Nah, we're not." Jace spoke good-naturedly, then added as an afterthought, "Unless you break our sister's heart."

"I'm not planning to."

A muscle jumped in my neck as I remembered what Val had said before leaving to buy pie. *Just ignore any sentence including the words serious or future, okay?* Was it just a playful warning because she knew there was a chance I'd be cornered? Or did she truly not want more from me than a good time?

My jaw ticked. I certainly wasn't planning to let her go.

Hailey appeared out of thin air next to me. "They're hazing you, aren't they?"

"They were starting to."

She glared at her brothers. Jace held up his hands in surrender. "We're your brothers. It's what we do."

"What he said," Will added.

Hailey parked her hands on her hips. "Will, I was expecting better of you. You're now in a happy relationship. I'd thought you'd cut back on the brooding. Instead, you're rubbing off on Jace."

"Sister, we're just doing our part," Jace volleyed back smoothly.

Hailey waved her hand, then turned to me.

"Don't pay attention to Jace these days. I think he's extra broody because he's still single."

Jace elbowed Hailey playfully. "You're single too."

"Or maybe not. Maybe I'm just not parading all my secret lovers in front of you."

Both Will and Jace looked too stunned to answer. Hailey took advantage of the opportunity, lacing her arm with mine. As we walked away, she looked over her shoulder.

"Oh, man, I was just trying to take the spotlight off Val, but I think I've just set myself up for months of questioning and them flexing their brotherly muscles."

I chuckled. "You're a great sister."

"Well, yes, I am, thank you very much. Though truthfully, Val and Lori paved the way for me in just about every aspect. Well, Lori mostly. Val was more like a mom to me growing up. I always felt a little guilty."

"For what?"

"For the fact that Val and Landon had to put their lives on hold for us. Instead of enjoying the freedoms of any college students, they were bogged down with... well, us."

"Hailey, Val never saw you as a burden. She always speaks with affection about everyone."

"I know. She's Val. But I know she's missed out on a lot of things. She tended to forget about herself, though she is getting much better at it lately.

In case you can't read through the lines... just make sure you dote on her, okay?"

"Yes, ma'am."

Hailey grinned. "You're great. But I feel compelled to tell you, if you break her heart, it's not my brothers you have to worry about. I know I don't look too intimidating next to them, but I can do a lot of damage."

"Duly noted."

"Ah, Val's back with the pie. Just in time."

Val was placing the pie on the small wooden table near the back door, but her eyes were on Hailey and me, then darted to Jace and Will, who were talking with their heads together.

We all wanted a slice of pie before the badminton game, and while everyone was eating, Val asked me to help her get some glasses.

"Did they give you the talk?" she asked breathlessly the second we were alone inside the house.

"Yeah."

She was beside herself, and she was damn cute.

"Holy shit, I'm going to kick everyone's ass."

"There's no need."

"Was Jace part of it?"

"Yes."

"And Will?"

"Obviously."

"But Hailey wasn't, right?"

I could tell she was hoping I'd say no, but I

wouldn't lie.

"She gave me some interesting insights into you, but warned me that if I broke your heart, then I don't have to worry about your brothers. That she can do enough damage all on her own."

She hung her head, eyes closed, like a sad puppy. "You have no idea how many points you're getting for still hanging around."

"I didn't know you were keeping a tally."

"I like my pro/con lists."

"I see. Pros outweigh the cons?"

When she nodded, I added, "Maybe you should share that list with them."

"Yeah, I…. Maybe not." Her cheeks went pink.

"Why, what's on that list?"

"Ummm… stuff they shouldn't see?"

"I want details."

She poked my arm. "You're not getting them."

"Oh, I am."

She opened her mouth, to argue some more, no doubt, but I kissed her before she even had time to make a sound. She was glaring when I pulled back, which only made me want to push her against a wall and sink inside her.

"So?"

"Are you going to kiss me like this every time we don't agree on something?"

"If that's what it takes."

"Then maybe we should disagree more

often."

I was speechless for a second but recovered and led her around the corner, then pulled her flush against me.

"Fondling me in public won't win you any points with them."

I brought my mouth to her ear. "They can't see us. And anyway, it'll earn me points with you, won't it?"

Judging by the way she attempted to hide her face in my shoulder, I was spot-on.

"I bet your pro column includes—"

"Activities of the X-rated variety, yes. Thanks for making me say it out loud."

"Now what would they say if they knew about that?"

She groaned. "They don't have to know everything."

"Don't worry. I'll keep your secret."

I drew the tip of my nose down the column of her neck, breathing in her sweet scent.

"New perfume?"

"Yes. Do you like it?"

"I do. You smell good enough to eat."

I pressed my hips against hers, and a moan replaced her laughter. She clutched at my sides with both hands.

"Fucking hell, woman. You make me want to haul you over my shoulder and take you upstairs. Distract me."

"The perfume is part of a new collection.

We're trying out a fresh concept, where we deliver the basic essence to the stores and then the customer chooses their own end notes to top it. I was thinking April and Peyton would love to play with this in our mixing lab."

I straightened, my pulse suddenly thrumming in my ears.

"Only if you're okay with it," she added quickly.

"I'm more than okay with it. I think they'll love it."

"I think so too. I've even thought about the selection for each." She snapped her gaze up, catching my expression. "What?"

"Nothing."

I didn't know how to put my whirlwind of thoughts into words, to tell her how much it meant to me that she'd given April and Peyton so much consideration. I couldn't be the only one who was deeper into this than we'd anticipated. My feelings couldn't be one-sided. No way, no how.

"We should go outside," I said. "Or they're going to suspect we're up to no good."

"Oh, they've been suspecting since I dragged you into the house. But let's not give anyone the opportunity to catch us in the act."

I chuckled, pressing her close one more time before we headed to the others.

I was going to go all out for this woman.

Chapter Twenty-Four
Carter

"April, tell me I'm seeing an extra zero." I was looking at the total price of her cart, aghast. Fifty-six items.

"Nope. I've cut down from one hundred and eight, by the way."

I glared at my niece hopelessly. She'd shown me the list some time ago, but it had grown exponentially ever since.

"How did you even find all these things?"

"Val advised. She also said you could talk to her if you have any complaints," she said with a self-assured air, as if that was foolproof. She gave me the same excuse the last time she shoved the list under my nose.

"Did she now?"

"Yep. And by the way, you'll be late for your date."

"And you conveniently showed me this just as I was about to leave?"

She gave me a sheepish smile.

"Also Val's tactic?"

"Yep."

"We're going to circle back to this another

day."

"But can I at least order a few?"

"No. I know what you're doing. It's not working."

April pouted. Jesus, I'd barely resisted giving in to April before. If she and Val teamed up, I was a dead man. Angela, the girls' nanny, was playing with Peyton in the living room. Peyton ran straight into my arms when she saw me, giving me one of her heartfelt smooches on the cheek. I hugged her close, kissing her forehead and reminding her to listen to Angela while I was gone, then I headed out for my date with Val.

I had quite the plan for tonight, and I was brave enough to admit I'd needed help putting it together. That help had come in the form of Hailey, who'd been ecstatic when I called her the morning after the dinner.

"I'm taking her out on a date, but I want to make it special. Any tips?"

"Holy shit, where to begin?"

Even though she was having breakfast with Jace when I called, she'd immediately started dishing information. Hailey gave me enough ammo for ten years' worth of dates. It had taken two weeks to put everything together for tonight. Her enthusiasm had made me grin, especially when under her breath, she muttered, "Jace, you can take notes too, you know. Every woman appreciates this stuff."

I'd heard Jace groan before saying, "Carter, you've just thrown me to the wolves."

Val had worked from home today, so I was picking her up from her house. The front door was open, and when I called her name, she answered from upstairs.

"I'll be right down."

When she descended the stairs, my tongue stuck to the roof of my mouth. She was wearing a red, strapless dress. It was tight and relatively short. She'd paired it with black high-heeled shoes. I would be fixating on them the entire evening.

She leaned into a kiss, and I grabbed her waist with both hands.

"Val, I can't go out of the house with you looking like that."

"Why not? You said we're going on a helicopter ride and then to dinner. Did the plan change?"

"No, it didn't. But you just look…." I took a deep breath. "Every man who sees you will want you."

She rolled her eyes. I tightened my grip on her waist.

"I want to be the only one who sees how sexy these legs are." I moved one hand to her inner thighs. Her breath hitched.

"How gorgeous these breasts are." I lowered my head to place open-mouthed kisses on the upper curve of each breast. When I straightened, I saw her nipples had hardened.

"Jesus, you're not even wearing a bra."

"You can't boss me into changing, Carter."

Her eyes snapped fire, and I captured her mouth before she got out another word. I rubbed my cock against her, barely restraining myself from carrying her upstairs when she whimpered.

"Carter!" She pushed me away and wrapped a scarf around her neck. It was long enough that the edges fell over her chest, covering her nipples. I groaned. I had a slight suspicion that Val didn't see herself as nearly as sexy as she was.

"I can't believe I'm finally going on a helicopter ride." Val's voice was full of excitement as we stepped out on the landing area and the helicopter came into view.

"Thought it might be a good opportunity to see LA from the sky."

"I've always wanted to do it."

"I know."

"You've been talking to Hailey."

"Guilty."

"Are you trying to impress me, mister?"

She had no idea.

"Just the two of us?"

"Yes. I didn't want anyone else along for the ride."

There was a small crew on the platform, and one of the guys was looking at Val with interest. I pulled her to me, kissing her right there for everyone to see. I didn't care who was watching. I wanted to stake my claim on her.

"Carter...." She sounded breathless as I took her hand, leading her to the helicopter. The pilot explained to us how things would proceed, and then we were off.

We both received headsets so the pilot could communicate with us easily, and to block some of the roaring sound. Los Angeles was breathtaking from above. It was the week before Christmas, and the city was lit up even more than usual.

"This was so amazing," Val exclaimed after we'd stepped out from the helicopter. "Did you enjoy it?"

"Yes. Even though I'd imagined it a bit different."

"Different how?"

"Well, I thought we could talk during the ride."

She grinned. "I thought so too. I hadn't realized it would be so loud. But at least we could focus on the view this way."

"Are you implying I would have distracted you otherwise?" I wiggled my eyebrows.

"Absolutely. You're a major distraction factor, mister."

"Come on, baby. We're not done for tonight."

Our next stop was the restaurant where we were having dinner. I'd requested a table that was as private as possible.

"You went all out tonight," Val murmured as we sat down.

"Only the best for my girl."

Val blushed.

"By the way, I know what you've been up to with April. She cornered me before I left."

Val smiled coyly, shrugging. "A girl has to do what a girl has to do. I think April and I are soul mates. We are shoe mates at the very least. The girl already has great taste."

"You two will be the death of me."

"We're certainly going to try."

We chatted about the helicopter ride while we ate and about the girls' trip to Val's lab last week. I didn't know who'd enjoyed themselves more: Val, or April and Peyton.

"Do you want to dance?" I asked once we'd both cleared our plates.

"I can never say no to you."

"I'm banking on it." I led her to the dance floor and slid a hand around her waist as a slow song started to play. I stroked my thumb across her tailbone.

"Carter, that hand is a bit low. I don't like it."

I could hear the smile in her voice.

"I'd say you do."

"I'd say you're cocky."

"But you're into it."

She sighed. "Yep. What can I say? Tall, handsome, smart, and cocky works for me."

My heart was pounding insanely fast as I pressed my cheek to hers in an intimate gesture. I could feel the rhythmic thumping in my ears. How much exactly did it work for her? We'd agreed we were exclusive, and everyone knew we were a couple, but I wanted to know if she saw a future for us, if she felt the same way I did.

I knew my life was complicated but also knew I could make Val happy. Not just in bed but outside of it too. I couldn't believe I was so unsure of myself. This wasn't like me. I hadn't doubted myself so much even during the most complicated cases. But I'd never stood before a woman about to lay out my feelings. I'd honestly never thought I would.

"What we have makes me so happy, Val," I whispered against her cheek. "But I care for you very much, and I don't want us to see this as just some fun time. You're on my mind no matter what I do or where I am. I want to share every important moment with you. Usually I'm not big on labels, but I'd like for us to see where this relationship takes us. What do you say?"

I felt her sharp intake of breath, and everything inside me stilled. Our cheeks were still pressed together. Say yes. God, say yes.

The wait seemed like minutes, when in truth, no more than a few seconds could have passed.

"I'd love to."

I'd never felt so much tension leave my body all at once.

"Yeah?"

She nodded, pulling back and looking at me with wide, uncertain eyes. "You mean everything you've just said, right?"

"Why would I say it if I don't mean it?"

"Because you think that's what I'd like to hear." She tensed in my arms.

"What are you afraid of, Val?"

"Hoping," she answered in a small voice. "I've always been a very optimistic and hopeful person. It's just that the things I hope or dream about most don't tend to happen... unless I make them happen. But obviously some things I can't influence...." She cast her gaze downward. "Let's just say I've tried to give away my heart a few times, but no one wanted it."

She'd said this very quickly, as if she'd wanted to get it off her chest. I'd never heard her speak so openly. I cupped her cheek, drawing my thumb along her bottom lip. Valentina Connor meant everything to me, but I knew we had to take this slowly. This was new, and we were treading on quicksand. If we moved too quickly, it would swallow us up.

"You don't have to be afraid with me. I promise." I kissed her, and she opened up to me in a way she'd never done before. Jesus, I wanted to ravish her right there on the dance floor. I held her close to me until the song finished, and then whispered, "Let's go home, Val. I want to bury myself inside you."

Her eyes widened, and her gaze fell to my lips. Then she licked her own and nodded. We were out in minutes.

The second we made it to her bedroom, I skimmed my thumb over her bare shoulder, then placed a kiss in the same spot. I wanted to map her body with my hands and my mouth, discover what made her wild with lust, and then I'd be the only one holding the key to her pleasure.

I captured her mouth at the same time I gathered the fabric of her dress in my hand, grabbing more and more until I felt the smooth skin of her legs under my fingers. I inched one hand upward between her thighs until my thumb reached her panties. She whimpered and then moaned when I pushed the fabric to one side, touching bare skin. She was so aroused that my control instantly slipped away. I almost took her against the door. I stopped kissing her only long enough to pull the dress over her head. Then I took care of my shirt while frantically unbuckling my belt. The rest of my clothes went away in minutes.

"Carter!"

"I want you so much."

I took a step back to admire her, sweeping my gaze over her body slowly, taking in every curve, how luscious that black lace looked against her pale skin.

I wanted to touch and kiss and stroke, but where to begin? Taking her hand, I led her from the door to the bed.

"Lie down on the bed, Val."

Her eyes widened as she first sat, then moved to the center of the bed, propping herself on her elbows. Her knees were pressed together, but when I climbed on the bed, I wrapped one hand around each ankle, moving them apart. I touched and kissed her legs, nipping at her inner thighs until Val gasped.

"Carter, please."

I smiled against her skin, inching ever so slowly to her center.

When I reached the apex, I moved onto her belly, continuing my exploration upward to her breast. I drew circles with my tongue around her nipples, occasionally sucking each into my mouth. She shuddered every time I did.

Her hands were everywhere: on my chest, my arms, my back. And then Val wrapped her palm around my erection, pressing her thumb on the crown.

"Val, baby!"

I watched as we stroked each other. I slid one hand between her parted thighs, in her panties, stroking one finger inside her, and then another one.

She cried out my name, and when I pressed my thumb on her clit, her inner muscles tightened around my fingers. I looked her straight in the eyes, not wanting to miss any change in her expression.

"That's it. You're so sexy. So responsive."

"Carter, you're going to…."

"I'm going to make you come, yes."

She clenched tighter, and her hips bucked off the bed. I used my other hand to press her pelvis against the mattress again, increasing the pressure. She pinched her eyes shut.

"OhGodohGodohGod."

She stopped moving her hand on my erection, as if the pleasure I was giving her was so intense that she couldn't do anything else besides surrender to it.

"Carter, I can't—"

"Yes, you can. Just let go."

My control was stretched thin, and it snapped when Val went over the edge with a primal sound, stretching out one shaky leg, pinching her eyes shut. I needed to be inside her right now.

***

Val

My breath was ragged, and I still hadn't opened my eyes, but when I heard Carter whisper my name, a shiver went through me, turning my skin to goose bumps from my toes all the way to my shoulders.

Anticipation built up inside me again. I'd just climaxed, for God's sake. The fabric of my panties was torture against my sensitive skin.

I opened my eyes when the mattress caved between my legs. Carter leaned over, hooking his thumbs at the sides of my panties. I lifted my ass just enough for him to pull them down.

He parted my thighs wider still, settling between them. Lifting one ankle, he placed it on his shoulder. He did the same with the other one. I felt his erection pressing against my right ass cheek before he gripped himself at the base. I thought he'd slide right in, but he just rocked his length along my entrance, a gentle move that drove me crazy. My center was pulsing like mad, and that pulse reverberated across my skin, lighting me up. Our gazes locked, and my breath came out in a rush. I felt as if I was laying bare more than my body, surrendering more than my pleasure. He was looking at me as if he felt that scary connection as deeply as I did.

I gasped when he slid inside me, filling me up so much that my insides strummed tight. He moved fast, and he seemed to reach deeper with every thrust, growing wider still. Every move brought me closer to another climax… or maybe I was still riding the wave of pleasure from the first one.

The muscles in my belly contracted, and when he skimmed his thumb over my clit, I grazed the bedsheet with my nails. I desperately needed my release. But Carter had other plans.

Pulling out of me, he flipped me around on all fours. I whimpered, missing the contact, that sensation of being full of him. He didn't enter me though, and I shifted backward.

He laughed softly, and then I felt his lips on my back.

"You miss my cock inside you already?"

I whimpered again.

"Yes." I wasn't sure he'd heard me, because the word had come out lower than a whisper.

He brought his lips lower, to the base of my spine, and lower still, to my ass cheek. Kiss. Bite. Kiss. Bite. Moving on to the other ass cheek, he applied the same sweet torture. Carter rubbed two fingers in wide circles around my clit without ever actually touching the sweet point. He was just lighting up the nerve endings but not quite setting them on fire. And his tongue was licking up the most sensitive part of me, where my string had covered me before. It was enough to turn me blind with need.

When he finally, finally thrust inside me again, I felt every inch of him more intensely.

"Fuck, you're beautiful, all flushed like this."

I'd pressed one cheek to the mattress, and he could see half my face. My burning face. When I brought one hand to my clit, I met Carter's fingers.

I took my hand away, using it for leverage, pressing my palms into the mattress as I thrust back into him, needing every last drop of pleasure. Carter worked my clit relentlessly while he pumped in and out of me. I'd never experienced pleasure so raw and all-consuming. My muscles burned and protested as I moved to the feverish rhythm. Spasms ricocheted through me as the tension circled closer to my center, the orgasm building up mercilessly.

I reached back with both of my hands to touch Carter's thighs, urging him to go even faster.

I exploded, my vision fading at the edges. When I felt him swell inside me a few seconds later, I thought I might shatter from so much pleasure.

After we cleaned up, we lay next to each other, Carter cradling me in his arms. I smiled against the skin of his torso.

"What's with the smile?" His voice was a mere whisper, as if he was still regaining his strength.

"I like that you're sweaty. And that you cuddle me." And that he'd wooed me with that spectacular date before speaking so openly about his feelings. Part of me still thought I'd imagined all that. I was a little ashamed that I'd laid out my insecurities, but when he'd asked what I was afraid of, I couldn't bring myself to feign nonchalance.

I nipped at his shoulder playfully, and next thing I knew, Carter had rolled on top of me again, pinning my hands above my head.

He did have some strength left after all.

"How do you do this to me?" He spoke against my nipple. I was about to ask what he was referring to, but then I felt his hard-on pressing against one of my thighs. I sucked in a breath.

"I can't believe you sometimes."

He lifted his head, looking straight at me. He'd taken that as a challenge.

God help me.

Chapter Twenty-Five
Val

The holiday season was always a bit crazy in the Connor clan. Carter and the girls spent Christmas with us the next week, and introducing April and Peyton to my family was simply precious. Peyton had been shy and silent in the beginning but opened up when she realized everyone had a present for her. April was starstruck by Jace. She wasn't a soccer fan, but she'd started following him on social media after his newest GQ title. I'd overheard her inform Carter later that evening that he was officially a "cool uncle" because he knew Jace.

At the next Friday dinner, April asked my brother for an autograph. It took yet another week for her to work up the courage to ask him to take a photo with her, but now I could confidently say the girls felt comfortable around the Connor clan... which was why I was certain they wouldn't be overwhelmed when I introduced them to two of my Bennett cousins.

My cousins Pippa and Sebastian were in LA. Since they were flying back to San Francisco tomorrow morning, they couldn't make it to our traditional Friday dinner, so I'd invited them over today, on a Thursday.

I was picking up Peyton and April from school, then going to my house with them.

None of my siblings could stop by, unfortunately, but that gave me a chance to brag about my man and the girls.

After picking them up from school, I headed directly home. Carter was meeting us there.

On the way, the girls talked my ear off.

"So, I don't know what to do," April said thoughtfully. "Should I text him back? Or not?"

"Go for it."

April grinned at me. "I will."

Peyton had other issues. "Val... I need a costume for the festival. Can you come shopping with us? Pleaaaase."

"The festival is next Tuesday, right?" Since Carter and I were actively trying to shift things around in our lives to make time for each other, I also had a copy of the girls' schedule.

"Yep."

"We'll go shopping Saturday, okay?"

Peyton clapped her hands, nodding excitedly. Carter was already at my house when we arrived. I'd offered to pick up the girls because their school was on my way from a meeting. I loved spending time with them and goofing around. We'd grown closer since that swoon-worthy night with Carter.

The girls and I also plotted behind Carter's back quite often, which was probably why he scrutinized us as if we were in the witness box when he saw us.

"What secrets are you keeping from me this time?" he asked.

"No secrets. We're just going shopping on Saturday to buy a costume for Peyton," I replied smoothly.

He grimaced. "Got it. I'm in for a few hours of torture."

April rolled her eyes, heading inside the house with Peyton. I took advantage of the fact that we were alone and whispered, "I promise to reward you very generously after the shopping trip."

Ah, that glint in his eyes was simply delightful.

My Bennett cousins arrived shortly afterward, and we ordered in dinner.

They were in town on a business trip for their company, Bennett Enterprises. They made the most beautiful jewelry, and they were in talks with Blair, one of Hollywood's hottest leading ladies, to have her be the face of the company.

Sebastian was the CEO, and Pippa the head designer. Out of the nine siblings, five worked at Bennett Enterprises. I was always eager to catch up with them. Over the past few years most reunions had been at weddings (all nine of them were married), or when they had business here.

"Such a pity no one else could make it," I commented.

Pippa waved her hand. "Everything was too short notice, but we wanted to meet Blair before we signed her, to see how she is as a person."

"We've never had someone represent the company this way. It's a big risk, but she has international recognition—in Europe especially," Sebastian continued.

"Taking over the world, huh? I will forever be in awe of the way your brain works," I told Sebastian honestly.

"I'm not doing it on my own. Everyone works hard."

"He just likes being modest from time to time," Pippa mocked.

"My wife would disagree with you."

"I can't believe Ava actually agreed to share an office with you."

Sebastian grinned wolfishly. "What? I am the CEO. If I want to share an office with my marketing director, who also happens to be my wife, why shouldn't I? It makes perfect sense. Many synergies in our work."

"Uh-huh. That's why it took you years to convince Ava. Because those synergies will be so productive." Pippa chuckled, but her eyes flew to April and Peyton, and I knew that if there hadn't been kids at the table, she would have called him out on the tactic. I imagined those synergies included some hot make-out sessions... at the very least.

"By the way, I saw that Jace is in one of your social media campaigns," Pippa said.

I grinned. "He is. And he's killing it."

"Pity he's not here." Pippa flashed one of her trademark "I'm plotting" smiles. She liked to tease

Jace relentlessly.

I went on to pepper Sebastian and Pippa with questions about their international endeavors. I was curious, but business talk made me nervous. I'd hoped the litigation with Beauty SkinEssence would be resolved before it went to trial, but to no avail. We had the trial date in six weeks. I was getting more nervous by the day.

But for tonight, I resolved to shove the issue to the back of my mind and enjoy my cousins and my man.

***

On a bright Tuesday morning two weeks later, I found Anne close to tears at her desk.

"What's wrong?" I asked.

"You didn't read it?"

"Read what?"

She turned her monitor to me, and my heart sank. A business publication had written an article about the upcoming lawsuit, and it wasn't painting me in a pretty light. They used terms like fraud and foul play. A source inside Beauty SkinEssence had given them their side of the story, but since the publication hadn't asked for mine, it was clear this wasn't impartial journalism. It was a smear campaign led by Beauty SkinEssence.

Despite the fact that a chill of panic raked through me, I set my hand soothingly on Anne's shoulder.

"This doesn't mean anything, Anne. The judge will decide, not the press."

I wanted to set an example for my employees, and I needed them to know they could trust me to lead them even through difficult times.

But over the next week, my leadership skills were put to test like never before. Three other business publications picked up the story, and since only Beauty SkinEssence's side of the story was available, that's the one they highlighted.

As a PR pro, Hailey was my counselor.

"Call journalists and give them your side."

"I plan to do that, but I also want to do more."

In the end, I contacted each journalist and posted an open letter on my company's website, which I penned myself under Hailey's supervision. Some of the journalists said they would mention my statement, some were skeptical.

What gnawed at me was that these publications were respected in business circles, and a judge might believe that what they were reporting were facts, not suppositions.

Apparently, my lawyer thought the same thing.

"You can't be serious. The trial is in three weeks," I barked into the phone.

"Ms. Connor, I'm sorry, but... my current health does not permit me to continue with my current workload."

"Why don't you tell me what's really going on?"

"The case is receiving too much attention, and if the judge will not rule in your favor… our firm doesn't want that kind of negative press."

"I'll give you negative press," I said through gritted teeth. "You think it's going to look good for you that you dump your clients when you can't win a case?"

"Bowing out is preferable to losing."

"That's a very shitty company policy."

Anger coiled through me, and I tried to relieve it by squeezing the little stress ball Hailey had brought me a few days ago. It wasn't helping.

I barely ended the call when Landon's name appeared on the screen. Sometimes I wondered if he could feel when I was upset, because he always had uncanny timing.

"How is it going?" he asked.

"Well, I'd like to tell you I have good news, but my lawyer just dropped the case."

He went on to call my ex-lawyer every profanity in the book as I told him what had happened.

"I'll cast my net wide. We work with many lawyers on our deals."

"Thanks. You do that. I have a meeting starting in ten minutes that will last the entire afternoon, but I'll talk to Carter first. He's in the industry and might have some recommendations."

Chapter Twenty-Six
Carter

"Carter, come on. Don't take the Connor case," Anthony said.

I'd asked my two partners into our meeting room to let them know what I was planning to do.

"I'm not asking for permission."

I'd made up my mind the second Val texted me, asking me for lawyer recommendations because hers dropped the case. I'd missed her call because I'd been with a client, and she was in a meeting now, but I'd talk to her afterward.

"The case is too public," Anthony continued. "And the trial date is in three weeks. If you lose, it'll cost us a lot of business."

"I am not planning to lose it. And again, I'm not asking for permission."

"We're all partners in this," Zachary reminded me. "You can't put our reputation on the line for some woman you're dating."

No one spoke for a few seconds. I could already feel a vein pulsing in my temple.

"Zachary, I'd shut up now if I were you," I said dangerously. Val wasn't just some woman.

"Look, Carter, I wouldn't touch this with a

ten-foot pole," Anthony added. "We can't stop you if you want to take the case, but is she really worth the risk?"

"Yes. Yes, she is."

I wanted to take on Val's case. I wanted to fight on her behalf. I was a damn good lawyer. I couldn't just stand by as she went through this mess. I dropped by her office around the time she'd told me her meeting would end.

It was apparent that everyone except Val had left. I found her sitting on her desk. I could only see her back, but she was obviously tense. Her spine was straight, and her shoulders looked stiff. She'd been talking on the phone, but she must have heard me come in because she muttered a quick "I'll call you later" before placing the phone on the table and glancing at me over her shoulder.

I went straight to her, hooking an arm around her waist and bringing her to the edge of the desk. Then I kissed her, deep and slow. She kissed me back, reluctantly at first, but as I demanded more, Val gave in, releasing a small moan against my mouth, burying one hand in my hair and pressing her heels into the backs of my thighs, urging me closer. I wanted to wring out every single drop of tension from her, drive out all her worries.

I pulled back a little, tipping her head up.

"Hey," I greeted.

"Hey."

"What have you been up to?"

"Regrouping, mostly. Landon found a few law firms, but the ones I've spoken to are reluctant to jump in so late. Have you thought about any recommendations?"

Right. She'd texted me to ask for recommendations. I'd completely forgotten.

"Val, I want to represent you. I want to be your lawyer."

She blinked up at me. "What?"

Okay, so I'd expected a more enthusiastic reaction.

"I know you said we should keep the professional and personal separate, but the situation has changed."

"I know, but what about your firm? Have you talked to your partners?"

"I informed them, yes. They weren't thrilled, for the same reasons your previous lawyer gave you. I don't really give a damn. Why are you hesitating? Why didn't you even ask me to be your lawyer?" My voice was harsh, but I was a little pissed that she hadn't even considered it.

My heart was racing as I considered all possibilities. The lawyer in me wondered if she didn't trust my abilities. The man in me was fearing that she wanted to keep the lines between professional and personal intact because her feelings didn't run as deep as mine did.

"It's a risky move for you, Carter. I didn't think it would be fair to ask you."

She started twiddling her thumbs in her lap.

"I'm offering."

"I've just...." She trailed off and took a deep breath before continuing. "No one outside of my family has ever wanted to put themselves on the line like this for me."

"Val, I want to fight for you. I want to win this for you. Just say yes."

She nodded, and I released a breath, leaning closer, feathering my lips over hers.

"Should we start right away?" she asked.

"No. I'll wake up early tomorrow and look over all the documents. But tonight, I want you to forget about everything, okay?"

"Okay. Thank you for taking the case. And for being here for me."

"This is my place. Next to you. For the good and the bad. It's not all going to be smooth sailing, but you can count on me through all the ups and downs. I promise you can count on me."

"Thank you."

Her voice was a little shaky, as if she feared the idea just as much as she wanted it. I understood her perfectly. We'd both been through the wringer before, and it had ended up in either heartbreak or disappointment, or both.

"So, how are you going to make me forget about everything?"

"You mean my natural charm isn't enough?" I wiggled my eyebrows at her.

She grinned. "I don't know. I think you should up your game."

"I see. Are you sure you can take it?"

I slid a hand under her skirt, placing it midthigh. Her eyes flared, and she licked her lips.

"Hmm… maybe I shouldn't trust such a devious man after all. Your mind is always wandering into dirty territory."

I tilted my head. "Not this time."

"Really? What's your hand doing under my skirt, then?"

"The first step in helping you relax. That's on the agenda tonight."

"No, no. I owe you some quality relaxation time." She narrowed her eyes playfully. "In fact, I know what would make both of us relax."

"Care to share?"

"Nah, I think I'll torment you for a while."

I promptly attacked, withdrawing my hand from under her skirt and leaning closer. She leaned back at my abrupt approach, balancing herself on her hands. I saw my opening then and tickled her armpits.

Val laughed wholeheartedly. I was so proud I'd made her laugh tonight.

"Stop, stop, stop."

"Still not sharing?"

She shook her head. I changed tactics, bracing my hands on her waist instead.

I ran the tip of my nose up and down her neck. She shuddered, and I took immense pleasure at the way her body reacted to me. Her hips slid forward an inch, as if searching for me. When I cupped her bra over her shirt, drawing circles around the peak, she arched her lower back, moaning.

"I'll make you tell me," I promised.

"Oh, I know you will."

Chapter Twenty-Seven
Carter

I dove headfirst into the documentation, reviewing every single detail, then double-checking my own work. I did this in addition to the existing workload, which meant I worked late into the night and woke early in the morning.

Even when I'd been a broke student taking on every odd job available, I'd never had so much on my plate. The last thing I needed was the news Mom dropped on me.

I was eating lunch at a food truck close to the courthouse when she called. Seeing her name on the screen took me by surprise because she usually called in the evening.

"Mom, everything okay?" I asked the second I picked up the phone.

"Yes and no. We need to talk."

"Did something happen to you? Or Dad?"

"No, nothing of that sort."

"Okay."

I was standing at one of the small tables around the food truck and placed a palm over my free ear to block out the traffic noise.

"Shoot."

"I've been thinking a lot, and… I can't come back to LA, Carter."

"What?"

"Your dad needs me here. His recovery is slow, and he'll need me even afterward. I can't leave him on his own for so long anymore."

"Do you want me to hire someone to help you?"

"No, that's not necessary. But I really can't jet between LA and Montana like I used to."

"You can both move here," I suggested. "Dad wouldn't even have to sell the farm. I can support you both."

"You know how stubborn he is. He wants to be here with the farm. We can always move the girls in with us."

"The girls stay with me, Mom. It's what Hannah wanted. What they want, and what I want too."

"I'm sorry to spring this on you, but I've been thinking about it for a while, and well… the sooner you know, the sooner you can make arrangements with the nanny. I know Angela will leave in the fall."

Actually, Angela had recently informed me that she'd be leaving a lot sooner than expected, because she'd received an internship at a center researching child psychology and she was starting next week. It put me in a tough place, but I'd released her from the contract, because let's face it, it wasn't an opportunity she could miss. I'd honestly been thinking about asking Mom to return sooner. I understood her decision, but I wasn't looking forward to adding "search for a sitter" to my to-do list right now when I was stretched so thin already.

I just had to grit my teeth and come through for everybody.

I broke the news to everyone that very evening. First I spoke with Val.

"Not much will change, Carter. You're already a big part of the girls' lives."

"I know." I loved the girls with my whole heart.

"And I'm here for anything you need. In case you can't tell, I have loads of experience. It'll come in handy, I'm sure. I'm going to whip up dinner while you talk to the girls."

I laughed, amazed at how she took all of this in stride. But then again, this was Val. She never complained about the cards life gave her.

I talked to the girls in April's room. The three of us sat on her bed—up until the point I told them their grandma was staying at the farm. Then Peyton stood on her tiny legs and wrapped her arms around my neck.

"She doesn't love us anymore?" The sound of her small, shaky voice tore at me.

"Of course she does, pumpkin. But her home is there, and Pops needs her. He can't be alone all the time anymore."

April was biting her fingernails. Peyton said nothing, but her little body started shaking, and then she broke out in sobs. Panic crawled inside me as I tried to soothe her.

"We're going to do fine, I promise."

"But what if we need Grandma?" Peyton asked after the sobs subsided. "What if we have girly questions?"

"You can always call her."

"But she might not answer," April said reasonably. "Can we ask Val?"

I really should have cleared that with Val before answering, but the girls were watching me with such hopeful expressions that there was no way I could say anything other than, "Yes."

"And if Val leaves too?" Peyton pressed.

Way to stab me in the heart, kiddo. I could tell how much they feared this. Hell, I feared it too. I felt as if I was standing on quicksand, and any second now I'd sink in over my head.

"Girls, whatever happens, I promise you we'll figure it out together."

Dinner was a quiet affair, and the girls went to bed straight afterward.

"Are you okay?" Val asked softly once we were alone in the living room, curled up on the couch together.

"I'm still trying to wrap my head around it, honestly. I'll have to look for a new sitter."

"I'll help you. And I know the girls' schedule anyway. We can share some of the tasks until you find someone new."

My gut clenched. "You're sure? I'm very involved in their lives, and without my mom... they'll look up to you as a female influence."

"I figured that. I can be an excellent mother figure, if I say so myself. You can ask my siblings for references."

I drew her into my lap until she was straddling me. "I don't doubt you for one second."

"Then what's the problem?"

I decided to lay all cards on the table. "This is too much."

Val's shoulders dropped. She shimmied further back, as if she was trying to get away from me. I could swear she'd become tinier.

"You... you want to take things slower?"

"No, Val. That's not what I mean. I don't want to take things slower. Sometimes it feels like I can't even breathe if you're not with me. But I'm well aware this isn't what you signed up for."

"I want to be part of your lives. Why would you think it's too much?"

"Early on when April and Peyton moved in with me, I had some bad experiences when it came to dating."

"Carter, if anything, the way you love your nieces, the way you take responsibility for them only makes me care more about you."

I cupped her cheeks, kissing her forehead and then her mouth. It started out gentle, but then the lashes of my tongue became more urgent as her words sunk in. She cared about me. She wanted me, Peyton, and April.

I brushed the sides of her breasts, then stroked her nipples until they perked up. I moved one hand to her ass, pulling her to me until her center collided with my erection. On a groan, I cupped the back of her head with my other hand.

"Wrap your legs around my waist."

She immediately did just that, and I lifted us off the couch.

She started taking off my shirt on the way. Once we were in the bedroom, I closed the door, pinning her against it with my hips, and pulled her dress over her head. She gasped when my erection pressed against the wet silk of her panties. Her fingers spasmed, then curled, her nails digging in my biceps.

I groaned, rubbing against her again, driving her crazy.

I bit her bottom lip as I lowered her feet to the ground, and then the rest of our clothes flew around everywhere. I was desperate for her and loved seeing that desperation reflected in the way she responded to my kisses and my strokes. When she was completely naked, I stood before her, kissing a straight line from between her collarbones down to her navel, then lower still. I licked her clit once before moving back up, kissing around her breasts before taking each nipple into my mouth and circling it with my tongue. Her knees weakened with every lash of my tongue. She reached between us, touching my erection. I pulsed in her hand.

Gripping her hips, I turned her around. I could see both of us reflected in the mirror on the opposite wall.

She braced her arms on the dresser in front of her as I kissed her neck and shoulders. I touched her breasts, rolling her nipples between my thumbs and forefingers. Tension coiled through my body, building and building.

"Carter, I need you."

"I know you do, love. But you're going to promise me something first."

I slid my erection between her legs.

"What?" she gasped.

"You're not allowed to doubt my feelings for you. You promise not to do that again?"

Our gazes locked in the mirror. I saw her fears and wanted to erase them. She licked her lips, clearly trying to gather her wits, but I wasn't making it easy for her. I began moving my hips lightly back and forth, and the feel of her ass against my pubic bone was maddening.

"Val," I beckoned, continuing the slow torture.

"I promise. I promise."

I pulled back a little, flipping her around the next second, slipping my hands under her ass, lifting her up. My cock was pressed between us, rubbing her clit. She whimpered as I carried her to the bed. I'd barely lowered her onto the mattress when I slid inside her, giving her every inch. Her thighs shook, her breath caught in her throat.

"Oh, fuck," I groaned.

My rhythm was hard and relentless, and she was coming apart fast. When her inner muscles started to pulse, I slowed the rhythm, bringing her down from the cusp.

She cried in frustration, moving her own hips faster—until I placed one hand on her pelvis, pressing her against the mattress.

"I'll make you come, love. I promise."

The message was clear. I was going to do it on my own terms, and she had no choice but to surrender her pleasure to me. I was completely still inside her as I strummed my fingers over her clit, bending to take a nipple in my mouth.

"Oh, fuck, fuck, fuck, Carter."

Tension started spreading from the points where we were connected, slinking through my entire body. I'd never felt an orgasm form so slowly. All my muscles tightened, and when I kissed her to cover her cry of pleasure, I gave in to my own climax.

Chapter Twenty-Eight
Carter

The weeks leading up to the trial were brutal. I was on autopilot most of the time, except when it came to preparing Val's case. The night before the trial, I only rose from my chair at three o'clock in the morning.

Val wasn't in bed, so I went to check the living room, thinking she'd fallen asleep there. I discovered her in Peyton's bed. My young niece was cocooned against Val, who had laid an arm protectively over her. They looked so sweet and peaceful together. The sight almost brought me to my knees. I wanted to have the privilege of this sight every single night. I'd never wanted anything more.

I took Val in my arms, and she stirred, laying her head on my shoulder.

"I fell asleep in Peyton's bed."

"I know. I'm taking you to ours. You smell like nutmeg."

"Mmm... the girls and I found a cake recipe and decided to test it. What time is it?"

"Three o'clock."

"So it's already tomorrow." She blinked her eyes wide, and I felt her pulse intensify as I lowered her to my bed, climbing in next to her. "I'm scared, Carter."

"Don't be. We're going to win. I promise." I kissed her cheek, descending to her neck. "Go to sleep, babe. I'm sorry I reminded you about it."

She fisted my shirt, breathing in deeply. I kept her close to me the entire night, thinking about the case. I wouldn't disappoint her.

***

Val

The morning of the trial felt as if it was happening to someone else. I went through the motions of getting dressed and eating breakfast, and before I knew it, Carter was pulling the car into a parking lot a few blocks away from the courtroom. I was sweating bullets. My palms were damp, and so were the hair roots at the back of my head. I tried my best to listen to everything Carter was saying, but my frantic panic made my pulse jackhammer in my ears, blocking out most of his words. I knew by heart everything he was saying anyway. We'd gone through the agenda for the day many times.

"Val," Carter said softly once we were out of the car. "Listen to me. It's going to be all right."

"How can you be so calm? You have a lot at stake here too. Your business partners are unhappy with you."

"I don't give a damn if they're happy with me or not."

"How? How can you not give a damn?"

"Because I focus on what's important. And right now, you winning this case is important. You are important to me, Val. The rest is just background noise. I'm a very good lawyer. I'll find solutions. Just try to focus on the positive side. You have your family behind you. And you have me, Val."

I melted in a puddle at that. He was rationalizing everything. I tried to do the same, but in all honesty, I'd always been rather emotional in these types of situations. All I could think about was that if things went south, my business's reputation would be tarnished. I stood to lose contracts and orders, and I'd be letting down my employees.

Not to mention, I would take an enormous financial hit if I had to drop the skincare line and the judge decided I had to pay damages to Beauty SkinEssence.

Carter would lose a lot too. I couldn't believe he was putting his skin in the game for me like this.

"It's not working, is it?" he asked.

I shook my head. Next thing I knew, Carter had captured my mouth with his, pressing my back against one of the concrete walls in the parking lot. Holy shit, this wasn't your usual have-a-good-day-kiss. It was so sensual and hot that I nearly climbed him.

"What are you doing?" I demanded when we paused to breathe.

"Taking your mind off everything while we still have time."

I laughed. "I'm afraid not even your excellent kissing skills can achieve that."

He narrowed his eyes, and then slipped a hand under my shirt, cupping me over the silky bra.

"Did you just fondle me?"

"I did. And if you keep this up, I'll do worse."

Oh my.... Judging by that delicious glint in his eyes, I had a pretty good idea of what worse meant.

"You are devious, you know that?" I pushed his hand away halfheartedly, then immediately wished I hadn't, because all my worries slammed back into me. But it was time to put on the big girl panties and face the music.

Carter kept a protective hand on my back all the way to the courtroom. My family was waiting just outside, and I smiled.

"I can't believe you're all here," I muttered, taking in the clan. Landon hugged me particularly tight.

"It'll work out, munchkin," he whispered. I pinched him playfully. That had been Dad's nickname for me.

"I know it will," I said with as much strength as I could muster. I didn't want to disappoint my twin.

Again, I went through the motions for the next half hour. Inside the courtroom, I barely glanced at Beauty SkinEssence's representative and their lawyer.

I sat as straight as possible, holding my chin

high. I'd been through so much worse than this. I wasn't going to let them sense my fear. I wouldn't be intimidated.

The lawyer for the plaintiff spoke first. As expected, he was ruthless in the presentation of the "evidence" and depiction of my intentions. Then Carter rose from his seat. Clean-shaven, with those sharp eyes surveying the jury and the judge, he effortlessly dominated the courtroom.

While the opposing counsel questioned me, I made a point of looking him straight in the eyes and keeping my voice as neutral as possible.

"As mentioned countless times before, we all follow trends and market demands and strive to meet them. Simultaneous product development is not unusual. This has been a campaign to intimidate me from the very start," I finished. I caught Carter glancing at me from across the courtroom.

I'd never felt as loved as in that moment. I felt his gaze wrap around me like a soothing hug, and for the first time today, my anxiety felt manageable.

Carter went on to present exhibit after exhibit to showcase the integrity of my company, as well as the timeline of the events. This was the culmination of weeks of work on his part, on top of what my previous lawyer had prepared. After countless case hearings, this was the final act.

Our proof was all circumstantial, just as the opposition's had been. The product wasn't patentable. In the end, it would be up to the judge to decide.

Chapter Twenty-Nine
Val

Ten days passed before a decision was reached. I was in my office when Carter burst inside, holding the papers.

"The judge ruled in your favor. They have to pay all your representation fees, plus a hefty fine for defaming you with that article."

I read every word at least five times until it sunk in, and then I jumped into Carter's arms. He laughed, holding me tight.

"Thank you, thank you, thank you," I muttered, surprised when he walked backward, still holding me.

"What are you doing?" I whispered. When he glanced down at me with that smoldering gaze, I had my answer. A delicious tremor ran through me. A sizzle followed as Carter closed the door, then brought his mouth over mine. Oh, God, this kiss.

After pulling back a notch, he drew his thumb over my upper lip, then my lower one. His eyes held the same warmth and emotion they'd held in the courtroom ten days ago.

"You've been fantastic throughout all this," he said.

"Me? You did everything." We hadn't spoken about the trial once it was over, because I hadn't wanted to drive myself crazy trying to guess which way the judge would decide. Carter drew me closer to him, the hand at my back sliding almost down to my ass. "You looked ready to rip off the opposing counsel's head. But... I have some insider information, so I know there's more than a ruthless lawyer to you."

"How do you want to celebrate?"

"Well... I'm going to treat my entire company to lunch tomorrow, and maybe I can get all the Connors together today for an early dinner?"

"Sounds good to me."

I knew everyone was waiting with bated breath to hear from me, so I started making phone calls right away.

Twenty minutes later, we had a plan. Carter went to pick up the girls from school and met me at the restaurant, which was half-empty when I arrived. Two waiters pushed several tables together to form a long one. My sisters arrived first, and they pulled me into a Connor sandwich hug as soon as they saw me. My brothers arrived soon after.

Everyone came with their better halves and the kids, so we were a huge group, but I did like to celebrate in style. Carter arrived last with Peyton and April.

April grinned at me, giving me a thumbs-up, and Peyton ran straight into my arms.

"Carter explained that the bad guys didn't

win. So you won't be worried anymore?" she asked.

"No, pumpkin, I won't."

She planted a wet kiss on my cheek. I ruffled her curls.

"Ms. Dodger said we'll have a bake sale next week. Can you help me make cookies?" In a lower voice, she added, "Carter always buys them."

I laughed, lowering her onto a seat. "We'll make cookies, don't you worry."

While everyone was busy choosing seats and glancing at menus, I pulled Carter toward the back of the restaurant, into a small corridor.

"Val?"

"I have to warn you. Even though you put your skin on the line for me, my brothers might still throw one or two uncomfortable questions your way. It's who they are. Don't take it personally."

"I told you I don't mind. And if they do grill me, I think they'll like my answers." He laughed softly, cupping my head with both hands. "You're an amazing woman, Val, and I love you."

I'd hoped, of course, though I hadn't dared to hope too much, just in case I was making it to be more than it was. "I'm not expecting you to say it back, but I wanted you to know."

I buried my face in his neck, smiling against his skin. "I love you too. So much." He wrapped me in his arms, holding me tight.

"I'm not going anywhere, Val. I'm yours."

I breathed in his masculine scent, melting in his arms. Then Carter brought a hand to the back of my head, tilting it so he had access to my mouth, and kissed me until my center pulsed. I clenched my thighs, but it was impossible to ignore the ache forming there.

"I can't wait to have you all to myself."

I shuddered at the sexy promise in his voice. "The party will last about three hours."

His gaze smoldered. "Three hours. And then you'll be all mine."

***

Carter

We returned to the group afterward. I couldn't keep my eyes off her. I liked to see her like this: carefree and happy. For weeks she'd seemed to be carrying a weight on her shoulders, and I was glad that was over today.

Val was successful. Many would like to take her down. I'd stand between her and anyone who tried—they'd see exactly how ruthless I could be. They wouldn't get past me.

She loved me. I had no idea what I'd done to deserve this—to deserve her.

Everyone was chatting animatedly as Val and I sat down. She looked furtively around the table, as if trying to gauge if anyone had noticed our absence.

Jace grinned, catching on immediately. "Don't worry, sis. We all saw you disappear around that corner. Will and I were betting on how long it would take you to come back. He actually thought you wouldn't come back at all."

Will groaned. Jace winked at his sister. "But I had a little more faith in you. I knew you wouldn't ditch us."

"Of course not." Val's cheeks went pink. She was adorable.

Hailey cocked a brow at Will and Jace. "You two are taking hazing to a whole new level."

"We learned from the masters," Jace volleyed back.

Landon cleared his throat from a few seats away. "Jace, I'm changing my mind about letting you give that speech."

"Way to have faith in me."

Val blinked. "A speech?"

Jace stood, taking a glass of champagne. The chatter around the table died down. "I know Landon is the speech master in the family, but I want to say a few words. We're all proud of you, Val, and we'll always have your back, no matter what. I hope you know that, but it's worth repeating. We're all happy things worked out today. A big thanks to Carter for stepping up to the plate and looking after Val. To Val and Carter."

Val's smile was a little wobbly as we all clinked glasses. I squeezed her hand under the table.

While we dug into our dinner, Hailey captured Val's attention.

"We're making plans for a girls' evening out right now. We haven't had one in a long time," said Hailey.

"I know. Things have just been a bit crazy."

"Well, I'm not taking no for an answer."

Val nodded, then said, "Okay. Carter, can you pull up the calendar app on my phone, please? My hands are sticky from the wings."

I took her cell phone from the table, pulling up her electronic calendar. Something wasn't right. Most of the events in the afternoon were crossed off. I swiped back to the previous weeks and saw most of her afternoon activities had a red line over them. Did past events automatically cross off? No, that wasn't it, because all the past events that were in the mornings still looked normal.

We still hadn't found someone to spend the afternoons with Peyton and April, which meant Val and I were alternating working afternoons from home. I'd insisted that I could work from home every afternoon, or April could watch Peyton on her own until we found someone, but Val wouldn't hear of it.

I'd been so lost in my hectic schedule that I hadn't realized she'd canceled so much.

"This evening here is free," Val commented.

Hailey clapped her hands, asking the rest of the girls at the table, and then declaring it a done deal. April was giving me the evil eye because she'd wanted to ask Val to let her tag along on girls' nights out, but I told her she could only ask after she turned eighteen.

I hadn't wanted to bring up the issue of her

canceled events while we were celebrating, but on our way to the car, I did address it.

"Val, I had a look at your calendar. You didn't tell me that you'd canceled so many of your afternoon meetings and events for weeks."

"Of course I did. I told you I'd make time."

"Yes, but you don't have to stop doing the things you enjoy."

"I'll just reschedule them."

She brushed off the whole issue, but I didn't feel as if anything was resolved.

Chapter Thirty
Carter

Over the next week, I paid closer attention to everything. I did my best to try to make sure Val didn't put herself on the back burner. She'd gone on that girls' night out, but she was still canceling not only social events, but also meetings.

"I'll just go next year," she said one evening as we slipped into bed, when I asked her if she'd bought tickets to a wine-tasting festival in Florida she'd told me about. She was smiling as she said it, but I still worried.

"Go this year. I want you to have fun."

"But I am having fun with you," she replied. "You happen to know how to keep me entertained." Lowering her voice to a whisper, she added, "And let me tell you a secret. You're very good at it."

I laughed, pulling her against me. "What would I do without you, huh?"

"You would miss me terribly."

"You think?"

"I'm one hundred percent convinced."

"You happen to be right."

I kept her close to me as her breathing evened out, even though sleep evaded me.

A few days later, I arrived home particularly late. I'd been convinced I would find Val sleeping, but instead she was on the couch, bent over a stack of paper, writing furiously.

"Why are you up so late, pretty girl?" I kissed the top of her head, but she held out a finger.

"Give me half an hour. I'm in the zone, making notes for another potential line with Sephora. They mentioned they could see our collaboration becoming a yearly thing, and I'm bursting with ideas. I want to get them down on paper before I forget them. I didn't get to it this afternoon."

I sat in the armchair opposite the couch, watching her. She was magnificent, all serious and focused. Energy was rolling off her. I smiled but felt a pang deep in my gut as I remembered something Hailey had shared at the first Friday dinner I'd attended, about how Val used to only have time to work on her ideas late at night.

I swallowed, discovering a lump in my throat.

I knew better than to bring it up. She'd done nothing but appease me every time I did. I was going to change tactics.

Which was why, the next evening, I sneaked up on her in the kitchen after I put Peyton to bed. I stopped in the doorway, watching her. She was wearing sweatpants and a tight top, and her hair was pulled back in a braid. She was also dancing, holding the spatula like a microphone. I laughed. She whirled around to me, startled.

"I didn't hear you come up. Why are you laughing?" She parked both hands on her hips. "Not at my dancing skills, I hope. If you are, lie quickly. I happen to be very proud of my moves."

"Slow down, woman. I'm not laughing at anything in particular. Just enjoying the view."

She gave me a smile before returning her focus to the oven, where a cake was baking. I walked up behind her, placed my hands on her hips, and whirled her around.

"I want to talk to you."

"Uh-oh. That sounds bad."

"It's not bad." I pulled out the voucher from my pocket, dangling it before her.

"What's that?"

"A surprise."

Excitement sparked in her eyes. She licked her lips, wiggling her eyebrows. "Gimme, gimme. I love surprises."

I took the voucher out of the envelope, dangling it some more. She was too cute, the way she kept trying to read what was on it. Then she snatched it from me.

"Tickets to the wine-tasting festival. And a voucher for a three-night stay at a hotel," I said.

"Oh, that's awesome. When are we going? After you drop off the girls at your Dad and Mom's?"

Peyton and April had a week-long vacation, and my parents had insisted I bring them over.

"No, this is just for you and whoever you want to take."

"You're not coming?"

"No."

"I don't get it."

"I'll stay with Peyton and April at my parents' while you're away. Then we'll have a few days to ourselves when you come back before I pick up the girls. You go to the festival and take whoever you want. Go with Hailey and Lori, or your friends. Make a girls' weekend out of it."

She looked at the voucher, then back at me. "Why are you so bent on me going without you?"

"I want you to go and relax. You have girl time to catch up on, and I think some time on your own will do you good."

Her smile froze. "What do you mean?"

"I know you like having your own space, doing your thing with your sisters."

She lowered her gaze to the voucher and stared at it for so long it made me wonder if she was really reading the details or was just avoiding looking at me.

"What is going on, Carter?"

"You've been bending over backwards for me and the girls for weeks. This is not okay. You need some time to relax."

She slid away from my grasp, walking toward the kitchen window, leaning against the windowsill.

"I see. So, it was okay for you to take on my case even though it was a risky move for your business, and it was also okay for you to work sixteen hours a day because it was on top of your other cases, but what I'm doing is not okay?"

"The case was temporary," I pointed out. She folded her arms over her chest.

"So, what, if it had dragged out, you would have jumped ship?"

"No, of course not. Look, it's not the same thing."

"Yes, it is. You were there for me when I needed you, and now I'm here for you."

I ran a hand through my hair, frustrated that I couldn't make her understand my point of view.

"You've told me that while your siblings were growing up, you had no time for yourself, and that you started to enjoy your work-life balance only a few years ago. I don't want you to feel as if you have to give this up." I took a deep breath, knowing that my next words would upset her... but I needed to say it, just this once. Otherwise, this fear would gnaw at me bit by bit. She was caught in the daily grind now, but what if she woke up one day and thought she couldn't do it anymore?

I'd had a few relationships explode in my face because I was a package deal, and I hadn't cared for those women nearly as much as I cared for Val.

She was the one.

Maybe it wasn't fair to lay this at her doorstep, but I needed to know with absolute certainty that she wasn't going to give up on us later down the road.

"Use the time at the vineyard to think about

all this, consider if it's really what you want. Are you happy?"

She jerked her head back, blinking rapidly. "Of course it's what I want. Why would you even say that?"

"Because it's taking a toll on you—"

"So I have to rearrange a few things, big deal. I've always known I will have to slow down someday if I want kids, which I really, really want." She stopped abruptly, dropping her gaze to the floor. "You don't?"

"Yes, I do. I do."

"So stop saying nonsense. I don't need to reconsider anything. I love you, and I love Peyton and April."

"Val—"

"Don't Val me."

I advanced toward her, but she skidded to the side. The message was clear.

"Thank you for the tickets and the voucher. I will use them only because I don't want them to go to waste. But for future reference, don't do this again. Don't decide for me. I don't appreciate it at all. Now, I still have to wait fifteen minutes for the cake to be ready, and I'd like to be alone, please."

Chapter Thirty-One
Val

Over the next few days, Carter and I treated each other too politely, the way you do after a fight when there are still unresolved issues, and you know the other person still insists on their beliefs, but you don't want to fight again. Our interactions were bordering on frosty, and I thought the girls picked up on it, which filled me with immense guilt.

I'd called Hailey and Lori the next morning. They had been ecstatic about the trip. The festival lasted two weeks, and the tickets were flexible.

Since Lori had weddings booked every weekend, we had to go during the week. Hailey had to ask her boss for time off. Two hours later, she confirmed she was up for it. Neither of them could miss work for more than two days, though, so I was flying out earlier to take advantage of the three-night stay.

My flight to Florida was scheduled on the afternoon of the same day that Carter traveled with the girls to Montana.

"Have fun with your grandparents," I wished the girls as I dropped the three of them off at the airport.

"Thanks, Val."

I squeezed them both in a tight hug until April snickered and Peyton squealed adorably.

"You have fun too, okay?" Carter murmured, kissing my forehead.

"Sure."

He looked as if he wanted to say something more, then simply shook his head, and off they went. I felt a growing pressure in my chest as I waved them goodbye. Afterward, I hurried to Carter's apartment to pack for my trip. I had to go to my house too, but since I'd brought a few essentials to his place, I'd gather those first.

I hated packing. So the first thing I did upon entering the apartment was turn on the music on my phone. My favorite songs always made everything better. Right then, though, they couldn't assuage the ache I felt beneath my collarbone. I massaged my chest, wishing things between Carter and me would return to normal. Even the goodbye at the airport had been a little cold.

I knew that while he was sorry he'd hurt me, he still thought he had a point. At least he hadn't repeated that insane point out loud. I was getting mad just remembering our fight and shook my head. I couldn't get angry again, or I'd start a fight with myself.

Since music wasn't helping, I decided on a new tactic and called my assistant while I made a sweep through the house.

"Anne, walk me through the to-do list for the

next three days."

"Are you multitasking again?"

"You know me."

She rattled off a mile-long list of tasks, concluding with, "And the contract was just delivered. It would be great if you could sign it before going out of town."

"Sure, I'll stop by. I don't know why we can't all embrace the era of electronic signatures," I mumbled. "Would save time, space, and trees."

I made no progress packing while I was on the phone, so I ended the call. Honestly, I'd just hoped talking to her would interrupt the incessant stream of negative thoughts.

It quickly became apparent that I'd brought far more than a few essentials to Carter's place.

God, my stuff was everywhere. I had clothes on almost every surface in the bedroom, and even on an armchair in the living room. My makeup and skincare products occupied two shelves out of three behind the mirror in the bathroom. My scrubs and hair masks were spread out in the shower. His shower gel and shampoo were squished in one corner. I even found some of my clothes in Peyton's room.

When had I taken over his apartment?

Had I made myself too comfortable? Been too intrusive?

Oh, God, I had, hadn't I? Taking over the girls' schedule, even getting involved in choosing a nanny. He'd repeatedly told me that I didn't have to take on so many tasks…. I'd thought I was doing a good thing, that I'd made myself useful. If anyone looked up intrusive in the dictionary, my picture would be right next to it. I'd been that way as a kid, and after my parents passed away, that trait had intensified. Partly because I'd needed to take charge of everyone's lives, and partly because it was simply my nature.

It was the only way I knew how to love. I went all in, involving myself in every aspect of their life.

I broke out in a cold sweat as for the first time since our fight, I thought about another angle. The voucher burned in my pocket. I tried to calm myself down. It had been a thoughtful gift. I forbade myself to dissect it and turn it into something it wasn't. But he'd also told me to use the time to think if I was really okay with this, if it's what I wanted. What if he'd asked me to reconsider if I was happy because he was reconsidering things as well?

Was this a gentle way of indicating he was rethinking our relationship? My heart almost stopped at that. It couldn't be. Carter didn't do gentle. He was determined and passionate. When he had something to say, he didn't mince words. But maybe he made exceptions….

I didn't doubt that Carter loved me, but maybe he hadn't counted on my intrusive nature. Maybe once that side of me became too obvious, he realized it overshadowed the happiness I brought him. Had I been too suffocating?

I sank onto Peyton's bed, hugging her teddy bear. It smelled of cherries, just like Peyton, and brought a small smile to my lips. My heart was heavy, though, and my mind full of questions and insecurities.

All I could see were my piles of stuff spread out everywhere. They weighed even me down. When I stood up from the bed, I swayed a little, suddenly feeling lightheaded.

I didn't even know where to start packing. I started in our bedroom, before remembering some of the things I'd thrown around in the living room. And all those shoes in the foyer... I'd forgotten about them. I made a mental inventory of what I'd have to pack for the trip.

As I looked around the bedroom again, my heart was beating so fast, I feared it was going to jump out of my chest.

Then I decided I was going to gather all my things, just in case Carter needed his territory back and hadn't wanted to hurt my feelings by saying it.

My limbs felt heavy as I dragged myself around the house, picking up clothes and random possessions. My eyes were burning, and my entire chest felt as if I was being squeezed by a tight corset.

I stopped by the office to sign the papers, and before leaving I descended to the lab. My head chemist was still there.

"Nicole, if you need any input, you can always call me."

Nicole shook her head. "I'll survive three days on my own. But, before you go, I do have some goodies for you."

She showed me two small vials, then sprayed a puff from each on a paper tester.

"Newly concocted today."

I held them to my nose, and immediately wanted to hug her.

"You so deserve a raise. These are fantastic."

"See? I can handle things around here without you. Now go, have fun."

Nicole handed me the vials, and I pocketed them before leaving. Sampling was one of my favorite things to do in the world, but even that wasn't enough to keep my worry from spiraling into panic as I headed home. I needed to drop off there the stuff I'd packed that I wasn't taking on the trip.

I took a cab to LAX, wishing my sisters could join me tonight, even though I wasn't brave enough yet to share my fears with them.

I was ashamed that I was allowing my insecurities to overpower me.

I ran a successful business, and I'd overcome many adversities in my life. My self-esteem was at a healthy level most of the time. Right now, though? My mind was a dangerous place. I knew that, but I couldn't help that it worked a certain way.

I worried myself sick, wondering if my meddling nature had pushed away the man I loved; if I had suffocated his feelings for me.

Chapter Thirty-Two
Carter

I landed at LAX at 3:00 a.m. The girls were with my parents until the end of the week, which meant Val and I would have four full days for ourselves once she was back. I'd missed her so much. I'd wanted to share everything with her: a joke Peyton made, a cake I thought she would like.

I'd barely restrained myself from texting her continuously so she could relax properly. She'd sent me a few pictures of the vineyard and the hotel, and I was glad she was enjoying herself. She deserved it.

And once she got back, I'd have her all to myself.

At my apartment, I went directly to the bedroom, planning to sleep right away. But I stopped in the doorway, taking in the room. Something was off. I glanced around. The apartment was far too orderly. Val liked to leave her things all around, which didn't bother me. The girls did the same. It made the place look lived in. Had she tidied up before leaving? Or had the cleaning company been in here in the meantime?

But they never moved the clothes, unless they were on the floor, and then they placed everything on the bed. No, this must have been Val's doing.

I looked inside the dresser. None of her clothes were there. Had she needed all her things on the trip? Unlikely. Val had brought enough clothes here for three people. My pulse sped up when I checked the bathroom. She'd had what had seemed like a million bottles of all shapes and sizes spread everywhere, and now they were all gone. I popped open the top button of my shirt, suddenly feeling as if I couldn't breathe right.

Why had she taken everything? She couldn't possibly need them all on her trip.

An impossible thought wiggled its way into my mind as fear clawed at my gut. Had she left me?

I gripped the bathroom sink with both hands until my knuckles went white.

That couldn't be right. We'd spoken every day. Our conversations had been short, and Val had talked longer to the girls than to me, but I hadn't thought much of it. Should I have?

Since our fight, Val had been a little colder, but honestly, I'd deserved it. I'd planned to pamper her like a princess once she got back from the vineyard and we could be alone, to show her just how important she was to me.

She hadn't changed her mind, had she? I moved to the living room and poured myself a glass of bourbon. I had told her to take the time and think if she was happy with the fact that I was a package deal, if that was what she wanted.

Had she discovered she wasn't happy after all?

Had she decided she didn't want the girls and me?

It seemed impossible. I remembered her fury the night I'd suggested it, the indignation in her voice when she told me she loved the girls. But maybe once she'd stepped away from the grind of the daily life and had some time to reflect, things became clearer.

I was still standing at the small bar, with my back to the living room, not wanting to see how empty the apartment was. I didn't want to register what it could possibly mean, because I couldn't handle it.

If Val wanted to end things, there were better ways to do it than just packing up her things and leaving. What was I supposed to tell the girls? Or was she going to do us the courtesy of sitting down with us and explaining everything? I didn't know which was worse. Hearing from her mouth that she wanted to bow out, or living with the uncertainty.

The girls loved Val. They counted on her. God damn it, I loved Val.

After giving up on love, I'd found her. And she'd become such an integral part of my life, of me, that I wasn't even sure who I was without her anymore.

"Carter Sloane strikes again," Zachary exclaimed the next morning. I wasn't in the mood to have any sort of conversation with him. I'd been up all night, unable to set my fears straight.

We were on a conference call because I'd

announced I was working from home.

"I should have trusted your gut. The Connor case was very good for us."

Zachary was reading the newest press coverage about the firm. I didn't bother faking interest. I wanted to get off this call as soon as possible. My head wasn't in the game today.

"By the way, we received a request for representation from... guess who?" With pride in his voice, he named a Fortune 500 company.

Right now, I didn't give a damn about that either, which was saying something, since I'd wanted an account like that since we opened the firm.

"That's good to hear," I said finally.

"What's wrong with you?"

"It's just not a great day."

I felt a hollow ache in my entire body, as if I was coming down with the flu. Hearing Val's name had only intensified it. After finishing the conference call, I made to open my laptop, then closed it again. I wasn't in the right frame of mind to work, damn it.

I kept staring at the empty apartment, driving myself crazy trying to find an explanation. I was overwhelmed by a bone-deep desperation I couldn't shake off. Not knowing was excruciating. Eventually, I broke down and texted Val.

Carter: Got home last night and saw that all your stuff was gone. Laundry day?

I gripped the phone tightly when the words "Val is typing" appeared on the screen.

Val: Not exactly.

A white-hot pain gripped me, as if someone had stuck a burning needle in my chest, pushing it all the way to my back.

Carter: What do you mean?

Val: My things were everywhere... I'd practically moved into your apartment, and we'd never discussed that. And I've been poking my nose in the girls' business a lot... I thought that maybe you didn't like that I was so intrusive.

I stared at the words. She had thought what?

"Intrusive," my ass.

I clenched and unclenched my hand before running my fingers through my hair. So I'd been correct in my assumption that she hadn't just taken all her clothes for no reason. Was this just an excuse to blow me off instead of telling it to me straight?

Closing my eyes, I leaned my head back, breathing in deeply. Was there a possibility that I'd lost her already?

No, it just couldn't be....

I forced myself to remain as logical as possible even as my entire body was constricting with panic. I'd known Val for months, and I could say with certainty that she wasn't one to play games. If she had wanted to end things, she wouldn't have just up and left.

Unless she thought it would be easier not to do it face-to-face.

Jesus, why was I jumping to the worst conclusions? Maybe because I'd gone through my fair share of disappointments. But so had Val, hadn't she? I reviewed the message. Her text read as if she'd given this a lot of thought. I knew my Val well enough to piece things together, understand what was going on through her mind.

Carter: We'll have a serious talk when you come back. I'm picking you up from LAX.

Val: You don't have to.

Carter: It wasn't a question.

I'd offered to do that before, but she'd insisted there was no need for me to endure the traffic. I didn't want to be apart from her a minute longer than I had to.

I counted down the hours until her landing and arrived at the airport early.

When Val finally walked out, I let out a long exhale. She was alone, because her sisters were returning with a later flight.

Fuck, she was beautiful in that bright yellow dress. I couldn't wait to get her home. I wanted to taste her mouth and her skin. I wanted to sink inside her until she called out my name and understood that she was mine. I'd show her exactly how perfect we were for each other.

***

Val

Without a word, Carter grabbed my luggage and my hand, intertwining our fingers.

"Hello to you too," I said. "Where are we

going?"

"To the car, and then my apartment. We need to talk."

My heart had been in my throat ever since our text exchange. He hadn't even made one move to kiss me, but he'd taken my hand. That had to be a good sign, right?

I took in the sight of him, all tall and handsome, walking with determined strides. God, how I loved this man.

The drive was a nerve-wracking and awkward affair. He'd said he wanted to talk, but he wasn't saying anything. He was so close, and yet he seemed far. To mask my growing restlessness, I started talking about my trip. By the time we entered the apartment, I was on pins and needles.

When he closed the door to the apartment, I blurted, "Carter, are you angry with me?"

He placed the luggage next to the door before turning to me. His jaw was tight. "What do you think?"

I swallowed, leaning back against the wall, looking down at my hands. When I heard him approach, I blinked up. He braced both palms on the wall, next to my shoulders. He was so close now that our lips were almost touching.

"I thought you were leaving me, Val. Do you know how that felt?"

My eyes widened. "Oh, God, Carter. I hadn't thought about that. I'm sorry. That was never my intention. I'd just thought…."

"What?"

In a small voice, I admitted, "I was afraid that maybe you'd asked me to reconsider things because you were reconsidering them too. I know I can be overbearing and poke my nose in everything, and... I mean, I practically moved in. We'd never even talked about it, but my shit was everywhere."

He unhitched his hands from the wall, cupping my face instead. He captured my mouth with his, and the contact electrified me. He was passionate and demanding, his tongue stroking mine until my hands were fumbling at the hem of his T-shirt, desperate to feel skin. Before I knew it, Carter had lifted me off the ground, throwing me over his shoulder.

"Carter, are you crazy?" I half laughed, half shrieked.

"You are driving me crazy."

He walked to the bedroom, lowering me directly on the bed, then climbing over me, pinning me to the mattress. His knees were at the sides of my thighs, his forearms caging in my torso.

"Trust me to love every part of you, Val, because I swear that I will. Forever."

I melted into him, wrapping my arms around his neck, holding him close. "I promise to trust you, but I want the same promise from you in return."

"I promise."

"You thought I left?"

He closed his eyes. "It was a weak moment. Won't happen again."

He kissed me again, just as urgently as before, then moved his mouth to my throat, descending to my chest. He'd somehow managed to gather my dress around my waist, and then he pulled it over my head. His gaze roamed over me once, and then he rained kisses on my collarbone, stopping at the ribbon holding together my bra cups and popping it open. He tormented one nipple with his tongue, the other with his fingers. I bucked my hips, but Carter pushed them into the mattress with one hand, taking control.

"As to the other part, you're right. We've never discussed you living here. Let's rectify that immediately."

"Right now?" I cried.

"I have the upper hand right now, so hell, yes."

"No, you don't," I challenged, even though my entire body felt ablaze.

He looked at me with a devilish smile, moving to kiss between my breasts. I kept my composure and quirked a brow to prove my point. In response, Carter nudged my thighs apart, settling between them.

"Back to our discussion. Let's make moving in together official. I don't care if we live here, at your house, or if we buy something new."

"I don't care either. I just want us to be together."

"I would walk into City Hall with you right now and marry you."

"You would?"

"Yes."

Oh, be still my beating heart.

"I'd love to," I whispered. "But I think Lori might kill us both. She's been mentally planning my and Hailey's weddings for years."

He laughed against my skin, then moved his mouth lower along my body until his jaw was pressing against my pubic bone, and then lower still, peeling off my panties. We were a tangle of limbs as we removed his clothes together. I went on a mission to map his body. I managed a trail of kisses to his navel before Carter pushed me on my back, aligning our bodies.

The tip of his erection was pushing at my entrance, and I needed him inside me so badly that I was close to begging. I rolled my hips, but Carter pulled back, smiling like the devil he was.

"You're too impatient. I want to explore you first. I've missed you."

Before I could object, he brought his mouth to one breast, his fingers between my legs. I gripped the headboard behind me with both hands at the first strokes of his tongue against my nipple. When he pressed his thumb on my clit, a spasm of pleasure rocked through me. My inner muscles pulsed madly.

When he finally, finally slid inside me, he did it so slowly that my thighs shook from anticipation, from the intensity of it all.

I wasn't going to lose him. He was mine. He wanted to be mine, to love me and be on the receiving end of my love.

I cried out when he slid into me those last few inches. I came apart at the seams one thrust at a time. Every sensation was magnified. I was feeling everything so intensely that I could barely breathe through the pleasure. My inner muscles tightened when I felt him starting to swell inside me. I climaxed so hard that my senses were off-balance, and I drew him into a kiss, moving in sync with him until I took him with me over the edge.

A few minutes passed before either of us spoke. We were both curled on one side. Carter had an arm around me.

"I've missed holding you like this. Watching you sleep, waking up and spying as you get dressed in the dark," he said.

"You spy on me?"

"Yes."

"Every morning?" I clarified.

"And every evening. And if you happen to change in between, I spy on you then too."

"Isn't spying illegal?"

"You're so fucking sexy and lovely that it would be illegal not to spy on you."

I shimmied against him and was startled when I felt his raging erection against my back. "Again?"

"I told you I've missed you. I'm going to spend the next few days showing you just how much."

"You're such a sweet talker. All to keep me in bed."

"You're holding it against me?"

I turned around to face him, hugging my pillow with an arm. "Umm, no. Is my lying here naked not enough proof that you've won me over with your devious plans?"

He rolled us over until I was under him, pressing every inch of that delicious chest against mine. "Nah, I'm going to demand more proof."

"I'm more than happy to provide it."

Epilogue
Val

"I can tell you're spying on me," I said one Friday afternoon a few weeks later, smiling as I looked over my shoulder. Yep, Carter was standing in the doorway to my bedroom. I was sitting on the bed, iPad in my lap, typing an email.

"This isn't spying, love. I was just... observing you."

"So you're not here to convince me to lock ourselves in the room and ignore the outside world?"

"I would if the movers weren't arriving in ten minutes."

I still couldn't believe this was happening. Carter and the girls were moving in here. Today. My house had three bedrooms, and the surrounding land was big enough that we could always expand. We'd chosen Friday as move-in day because the house would be full of Connors who'd offered to help.

I went back to composing my email, feeling Carter's gaze on me. When I heard the door close, I spun around to him.

"What are you doing?"

"Come to think of it, there's plenty I can do to you in ten minutes."

I grinned. "I so saw this coming."

"Really?"

"Uh-huh. A mile away. Why do you think I hid up here to write this email?"

"Who are you emailing anyway?"

"Davis's nephew. He's been abroad, but now that he's back he wants a face-to-face meeting."

Davis had been so impressed by the samples we'd presented to him that he asked us to fast-track the line we were developing for him so he could have it in stores a half-year earlier than we'd originally planned.

Carter climbed next to me on the bed faster than if I'd dropped my clothes.

"I see. The old man had better stop trying to hook you two up."

"He has stopped. I told him I have this amazing man who isn't too thrilled with his plan."

"Good." That one word had come out in a warning tone, as if he'd planned to add or else. I chuckled.

"What?"

"Nothing."

Carter narrowed his eyes, and the next thing I knew, he set my iPad aside, pulling me into his arms.

"I love you, Val. Meeting you has been my luck. Loving you for the rest of my life will be my honor. My joy. You have my devotion. All of me."

"And you have all of me," I whispered, my voice full of emotion as I curled my arms around his neck.

Ten minutes later, we had to hurry downstairs. I tried not to look too guilty as I smoothed my hair. Will and Paige arrived at the same time with the movers, and Jace a few minutes later.

It was early afternoon, so we had just enough time before dinner to arrange the boxes and a few furniture items, so the house wouldn't look like a storage room.

April and Peyton would be home in an hour. We'd finally hired a new nanny for them. She picked them up from school and spent time with them when Carter and I were busy with meetings. Truthfully, though, I liked slowing down in the afternoons to enjoy my time with the girls. My team didn't mind me working remotely now and then, and Carter's partners were supportive of him. Things between Carter's partners and me had been a little awkward, since I'd known they hadn't been too keen on him taking on my case, but I assured them I didn't hold a grudge. Everyone liked being on the winning side. It was how life worked. I especially enjoyed being on the winning side right now, as the magazine that had published Beauty SkinEssence's smear campaign had run an article on me, singing my praises. The line had come out last week to rave reviews. Since the competition's line had come out at the same time, my profits were going to be small, but I wasn't too worried. It was just how business decisions worked out sometimes.

A few hours later, the house looked semi

decent and the rest of the family had arrived. I slipped into the kitchen to prepare dinner. I was making fried chicken—Jace's favorite. I was usually very strict about respecting his meal plan, but some comfort food was in order right now because his team had lost a game.

April and Peyton were "helping." Translation: while keeping an eye on Peyton, April and I were strategizing how she could order some boots Carter would surely deem too "grown-up." They were not. I was still working on my persuasion skills in that area, so I considered taking one for the team this time and simply saying I'd ordered them for April as a surprise.

Carter was going to feel ambushed, but it was high time I introduced April and Peyton to the Connor ambush and intervention techniques. Peyton was still a bit young, but I had full confidence that April could pull it off. Girls had to stick together. As someone who'd always been surrounded by overprotective brothers, I knew the girls needed someone to champion their causes. I volunteered for the task.

April clamped her lips shut as Carter came to check on us. He glanced from April to me.

"What are you two up to?"

What? How could he know? Could he read the guilt on our faces? Crap, he was a lawyer. He was probably trained to sniff out guilt a mile away. So I resorted to one of my favorite techniques to distract him: talking his ear off.

"Want to taste the fried chicken? It's delicious."

"Sure. "

"It's Jace's favorite. His team just suffered a defeat, and I'm making this so he won't be grouchy. Grouchiness is contagious in my family."

"Because we live here now, are we your family too?" asked Peyton.

I stopped in the act of stabbing a piece of chicken with the fork, spinning around to face Peyton. Her eyes were wide, and she was looking expectantly between Carter and me. April had gone very still. Carter squeezed me to his side. "Do you want to tell them?"

I nodded, then lowered myself to my haunches. Peyton ran straight to me.

"Of course you're my family too."

"Grandma and Grandpa too?"

"Yes."

I'd met them last weekend, when they flew in to officially meet me and to see the girls. They were both great people. Mrs. Sloane definitely seemed to want to move to LA permanently. Mr. Sloane insisted he had to be at the farm, but I could see him melting a little every time his granddaughters insisted they wanted to spend more time with him.

I wasn't known for orchestrating ambushes and interventions for nothing, so I foresaw planning one or the other in the near future where the Sloanes were concerned.

Peyton snuggled closer, lacing her little arms

around my neck. I'd told Hailey last week that Carter and I planned to get married, so of course, the whole Connor clan knew the next day. But we hadn't told the girls yet.

"Carter and I are getting married."

Peyton squealed with joy. April looked between Carter and me with a smug smile before saying, "I already know. Hailey told me."

"You've made my favorite," Jace exclaimed when we were all seated around the table a while later. "You always know how to put me in a good mood."

"Maybe I'm just trying to bribe you." I cocked a brow, leaning into him and nudging his shoulder playfully.

"Aww, Val. You know I'm always at your service, like the dutiful brother I am." He gave me a mock salute. "Though I'll never say no to fried chicken."

Truthfully, I'd just wanted to lift his mood, but since he'd just offered his unconditional support, I couldn't let this pass.

"Would you be willing to do another campaign with us? This one is shaping up to be great."

Jace grinned like a Cheshire cat. "I know. Our PR person says they're calling me the face of success."

"Oh, dear God." Hailey shook her head mockingly. "There's a real risk this will go straight to your head. As your sister, I feel it's my duty to keep you grounded."

"Not before he agrees to another campaign," I admonished her.

"Val, of course I'll do it. Is it true they're also calling me a heartthrob?"

"Yep. Which is just a nicer way of spelling heartbreaker," I teased.

Jace shook his forefinger. "No, no. Big distinction. I like heartthrob much better. It's not judgy."

After Jace and I nailed down the details, Lori cleared her throat. "So... not to be a nag or anything, but do any of you have news?"

She looked from Carter and me to Will and Paige.

"No, Lori, we still haven't set the date," I said, fighting a smile.

"You know, the four of us should elope," Will said conversationally. Lori gasped.

The entire table started laughing.

"Brother, not even I would dare elope," Jace said. "For the sake of the family, you need to let Lori throw you a huge-ass wedding."

Ah... he had no idea what he'd just gotten himself into. Lori had confessed to me once that she believed Jace would be forever a bachelor. Now I could practically hear the wheels spinning in her mind. I had to warn my little brother.

"Careful, Jace, or Lori will start planning your wedding before there's even a bride in the picture."

Jace took one look at Lori and groaned. Which was when Milo, presumably tired of so much adult talk, said, "Uncle Jace, can you practice with me?"

"Sure, buddy. Let's go. I feel an ambush coming anyway. I prefer spending time with the younger generation these days. No one's calling me a heartbreaker or planning weddings."

"Yet. But I'm a fast learner," April replied impishly, sitting up straighter. I was so proud of this girl. Following in my footsteps already. I sighed, looking around the table contentedly. All my favorite people in the world were gathered around me. What more could I ask for?

"Carter, you're going to have your hands full by the looks of it," Landon commented.

Carter winked at me. "I can handle my ladies."

Hours later, after everyone left, the house was quiet. The girls had gone to bed. When Carter went to check on Peyton, I was alone in the living room and seized the moment, taking out my phone and ordering those boots I promised April. The website was a pain in the ass. It took forever to place the order. I was just moving from the shopping cart to the payment page when a muscular arm wrapped around my waist. I threw the phone on the couch, but I was fairly certain Carter had caught a glimpse of the screen.

I whirled around, lacing my arms around his neck. He feathered his lips along my jawline, keeping me so close that our hips were touching.

"Wait until we're upstairs to unleash your seductive charms on me, mister."

"Why? So you can sneak behind my back some more?"

Oh crap.

"I was doing no such thing."

"Val." His voice held a note of warning, but then I felt him smile against my cheek. "I'll pretend I haven't seen the website."

"I like you more and more every day."

"Is that why you're siding with April?"

"No, but the girls need someone on their side." I pulled back a notch, looking him straight in the eyes so he knew I meant it.

"You really know how to keep me on my toes. And you're right, they do need someone on their side. Thank you for caring so much about them. It means a lot to me."

He placed both my hands on his chest. I could feel his heart beating rapidly under my palms. "I love you so much."

"I can't believe I'm so lucky," I murmured. He bit my lower lip gently before moving his mouth over mine, demanding full surrender. One hand gripped my hip possessively, pressing me harder against his pelvis. We walked backward until the backs of my knees touched a soft surface, then we tumbled onto the couch, laughing.

"We're going to have a happy life together, Val."

I shimmied under him, overwhelmed by the emotion in his voice.

"Yes, we are. I promise."

He smiled before lowering his head, drawing the tip of his nose over my neck. "Does that promise also include you keeping me on my toes every day?"

"Um... the answer to that will always be yes."

"And you're not even sorry, are you?"

"Not one bit."

"If you surrender to me so beautifully every evening, I won't complain."

I grinned, shifting and biting his earlobe slightly. "I believe we have a deal."

Other Books by Layla Hagen

The Connor Family Series

Book 1: Anything For You

Hotshot CEO Landon Connor has many talents. He's successful and driven, and maybe a little too career-focused. Some (like his big and boisterous family) would even call him a workaholic. Landon has good reasons for putting his personal life on hold...

But meeting landscape designer Maddie Jennings makes him question his choices. He can't get enough of her sweetness, or her sensual curves. Maddie Jennings is all he sees, and everything he wants.

Maddie hasn't met anyone quite like Landon. He's sexier than anyone has the right to be, and more intense too. He's a little bossy, a lot hot. Despite fanning herself every time he comes near her, she tries to ignore their attraction. Maddie isn't sure that she and Landon are quite right for each other.

When Landon romances her with late night walks and sinful dancing, she can't help giving in to him. His touch is intoxicating, and their passion is scorching hot. His love is beautiful

But can Landon open up his heart for longer than a summer?

AVAILABLE ON ALL RETAILERS.

Book 2: Wild With You

Wedding organizer Lori Connor loves her job. Planning people's happy ever afters have catapulted the single mother to success. When she meets the best man at the latest wedding, sparks fly. Graham Frazier is more than Lori has bargained for.

The charismatic soccer club owner is disillusioned by marriage after his divorce. He's also hot as sin... and kisses like a dream. Graham's touch is sizzling. Soon, he bosses her into accepting gifts and spending the night at his house (his excuse is good: she can't possibly drive after working a wedding, can she?).

Graham pursues her relentlessly, wanting those long legs wrapped around him and her smooth skin under his lips.

Then he meets her son, and that boy charms him even faster than his mother did. Before Graham know it, Lori's son has him wrapped around his little finger.

But are Lori and Graham ready for their lives to intertwine in ways they haven't even imagined before?

AVAILABLE ON ALL RETAILERS.

Book 3: Meant For You

Will Connor lives his life by simple rules: take care of those he loves, give one hundred percent to his job, and never ignore his instincts. So when he meets Paige, he doesn't plan to ignore their crazy chemistry, or the way her pretty smile strips him of all defenses...

As the development director of a non-profit, Paige Lamonica has met her fair share of people. But Will is something else entirely. The hot detective is a little too confident, and far too easy on the eye. She loves that he goes toe-to-toe with her at every turn.

When Will asks her to attend his sister's wedding with him, she thinks he just wants to throw off his scent some relatives with a penchant for matchmaking.

She couldn't be more wrong. Will wants her.

When she teases him, he teases her right back. When she pushes his buttons, he repays her with scorching hot kisses.

Paige discovers that there's more to Will than she thought. With every layer she peels off, she craves more...

But as the daughter of an army man, Paige has never wanted to get involved with someone on the force. Can Will persuade her to give in to their growing love?

AVAILABLE ON ALL RETAILERS.

The Bennett Family Series

Book 1: Your Irresistible Love

Sebastian Bennett is a determined man. It's the secret behind the business empire he built from scratch. Under his rule, Bennett Enterprises dominates the jewelry industry. Despite being ruthless in his work, family comes first for him, and he'd do anything for his parents and eight siblings— even if they drive him crazy sometimes. . . like when they keep nagging him to get married already.

Sebastian doesn't believe in love, until he brings in external marketing consultant Ava to oversee the next collection launch. She's beautiful, funny, and just as stubborn as he is. Not only is he obsessed with her delicious curves, but he also finds himself willing to do anything to make her smile. He's determined to have Ava, even if she's completely off limits.

Ava Lindt has one job to do at Bennett Enterprises: make the next collection launch unforgettable. Daydreaming about the hot CEO is definitely not on her to-do list. Neither is doing said CEO. The consultancy she works for has a strict policy—no fraternizing with clients. She won't risk her job. Besides, Ava knows better than to trust men with her heart.

But their sizzling chemistry spirals into a deep connection that takes both of them by surprise. Sebastian blows through her defenses one sweet kiss and sinful touch at a time. When Ava's time as a consultant in his company comes to an end, will Sebastian fight for the woman he loves or will he end up losing her?

AVAILABLE ON ALL RETAILERS.

Book 2: Your Captivating Love

Logan Bennett knows his priorities. He is loyal to his family and his company. He has no time for love, and no desire for it. Not after a disastrous engagement left him brokenhearted. When Nadine enters his life, she turns everything upside down.

She's sexy, funny, and utterly captivating. She's also more stubborn than anyone he's met...including himself.

Nadine Hawthorne is finally pursuing her dream: opening her own clothing shop. After working so hard to get here, she needs to concentrate on her new business, and can't afford distractions. Not even if they come in the form of Logan Bennett.

He's handsome, charming, and doesn't take no for an answer. After bitter disappointments, Nadine doesn't believe in love. But being around Logan is addicting. It doesn't help that Logan's family is scheming to bring them together at every turn.

Their attraction is sizzling, their connection undeniable. Slowly, Logan wins her over. What starts out as a fling, soon spirals into much more than they are prepared for.

When a mistake threatens to tear them apart, will they have the strength to hold on to each other?

AVAILABLE ON ALL RETAILERS.

ONLY WITH YOU

Book 3: Your Forever Love

Eric Callahan is a powerful man, and his sharp business sense has earned him the nickname 'the shark.' Yet under the strict façade is a man who loves his daughter and would do anything for her. When he and his daughter move to San Francisco for three months, he has one thing in mind: expanding his business on the West Coast. As a widower, Eric is not looking for love. He focuses on his company, and his daughter.

Until he meets Pippa Bennett. She captivates him from the moment he sets eyes on her, and what starts as unintentional flirting soon spirals into something neither of them can control.

Pippa Bennett knows she should stay away from Eric Callahan. After going through a rough divorce, she doesn't trust men anymore. But something about Eric just draws her in. He has a body made for sin and a sense of humor that matches hers. Not to mention that seeing how adorable he is with his daughter melts Pippa's walls one by one.

The chemistry between them is undeniable, but the connection that grows deeper every day that has both of them wondering if love might be within their reach.

When it's time for Eric and his daughter to head back home, will he give up on the woman who has captured his heart, or will he do everything in his power to remain by her side?

AVAILABLE ON ALL RETAILERS.

Book 4: Your Inescapable Love

Max Bennett is a successful man. His analytical mind has taken his family's company to the next level. Outside the office, Max transforms from the serious business man into someone who is carefree and fun. Max is happy with his life and doesn't intend to change it, even though his mother keeps asking for more grandchildren. Max loves being an uncle, and plans to spoil his nieces rotten.

But when a chance encounter reunites him with Emilia, his childhood best friend, he starts questioning everything. The girl he last saw years ago has grown into a sensual woman with a smile he can't get out of his mind.

Emilia Campbell has a lot on her plate, taking care of her sick grandmother. Still, she faces everything with a positive attitude. When the childhood friend she hero-worshipped steps into her physical therapy clinic, she is over the moon. Max is every bit the troublemaker she remembers, only now he has a body to drool over and a smile to melt her panties. Not that she intends to do the former, or let the latter happen.

They are both determined not to cross the boundaries of friendship...at first. But as they spend more time together, they form an undeniable bond and their flirty banter spirals out of control.

Max knows Emilia is off-limits, but that only makes her all the more tempting. Besides, Max was never one to back away from a challenge.

When their chemistry becomes too much to resist and they inevitably give in to temptation, will they risk losing their friendship or will Max and Emilia find true love?

AVAILABLE ON ALL RETAILERS.

Book 5: Your Tempting Love

Christopher Bennett is a persuasive man. With his magnetic charm and undeniable wit, he plays a key role in the international success of his family's company.

Christopher adores his family, even if they can be too meddling sometimes... like when attempt to set him up with Victoria, by recommending him to employ her decorating services. Christopher isn't looking to settle down, but meeting Victoria turns his world upside down. Her laughter is contagious, and her beautiful lips and curves are too tempting.

Victoria Hensley is determined not to fall under Christopher's spell, even though the man is hotter than sin, and his flirty banter makes her toes curl. But as her client, Christopher is off limits. After her parents' death, Victoria is focusing on raising her much younger siblings, and she can't afford any mistakes. . .

But Victoria and Christopher's chemistry is not just the sparks-flying kind. . .It's the downright explosive kind. Before she knows it, Christopher is training her brother Lucas for soccer tryouts and reading bedtime stories to her sister Chloe.

Victoria wants to resist him, but Christopher is determined, stubborn, and oh-so-persuasive.

When their attraction and connection both spiral out of control, will they be able to risk it all for a love that is far too tempting?

AVAILABLE ON ALL RETAILERS.

Book 6: Your Alluring Love

Alice Bennett has been holding a torch for her older brother's best friend, Nate, for more than a decade. He's a hotshot TV producer who travels the world, never staying in San Francisco for too long. But now he's in town and just as tempting as ever... with a bossy streak that makes her weak in the knees and a smile that melts her defenses.

As a successful restaurant owner, Alice is happy with her life. She loves her business and her family, yet after watching her siblings find their happy ever after, she can't help feeling lonely sometimes—but that's only for her to know.

Nate has always had a soft spot for Alice. Despite considering the Bennetts his family, he never could look at her as just his friend's little sister. She's a spitfire, and Nate just can't stay away. He loves making her laugh... and blush.

Their attraction is irresistible, and between stolen kisses and wicked-hot nights, they form a deep bond that has them both yearning for more.

But when the chance of a lifetime comes knocking at his door, will Nate chase success even if it means losing Alice, or will he choose her?

AVAILABLE ON ALL RETAILERS.

Book 7: Your Fierce Love

The strong and sexy Blake Bennett is downright irresistible. And Clara Abernathy is doing everything she can to resist his charm.

After spending her life in group homes, Clara yearns for the love and warmth of a true family. With the Bennetts treating her like their own, she can't possibly fall for Blake. That would be crossing a line...

But when Clara needs a temporary place to live, and she accepts Blake's offer to move next door to him, things escalate. Suddenly, she's not only supposed to resist the man who's hell-bent on having her, but the TV station she works for is determined to dig up some dirt on the Bennett family.

Blake knows family friends are off-limits, and Clara is more off-limits than anyone. But Clara's sweetness and sass fill a hole in him he wasn't even aware of. Soon, he finds himself gravitating toward her, willing to do anything to make her happy.

Blake enjoys bending the rules—much more than following them, but will bending this one be taking it too far?

AVAILABLE ON ALL RETAILERS.

Book 8: Your One True Love

She's the one who got away. This time, he refuses to let her slip through his fingers.

Daniel Bennett has no regrets, except one: letting go of the woman he loved years ago. He wouldn't admit it out loud, but he's been pining for Caroline ever since. But his meddling family can read him like an open book. So when his sisters kick up their matchmaking shenanigans, Daniel decides to play right along. After all, he built his booming adventure business by making the most out of every opportunity. And he doesn't intend to miss an opportunity to be near Caroline.

Caroline Dunne knows better than to fall for Daniel again. But his seductive charm melts her determination to keep her heart in check. Even with their lives going in separate directions, neither can ignore the magnetic pull between them.

But will they find the second chance they've both wanted all along?

AVAILABLE ON ALL RETAILERS.

Book 9: Your Endless Love

An incurable romantic with a chronic case of bad luck with men…

Museum curator Summer Bennett knows that happily-ever-afters are not make-believe. After all, her siblings all found their soulmates, so she's optimistic her prince charming will come along too…eventually. In the meantime, she focuses on her job and her volunteering—which brings her face to face with one of Hollywood's hottest A-listers.

When Alexander Westbrook flashes America's favorite panty-melting smile, Summer's entire body responds. When she asks him to get involved in the community where she volunteers, Summer is shocked that the Hollywood heartthrob agrees right away. Two weeks working side by side with the world's sexiest guy, and the game is on.

Far from the public eye, Summer discovers she likes the real Alex even more than his on-screen persona. Secret kisses and whispered conversations spark a fire in her that nothing can extinguish. If only his life wasn't splashed all over the tabloids…

Alex can't keep his eyes–or his hands–off of Summer. But she's too sweet, and too damn lovely to be swept up in his Hollywood drama. His career is at risk, and an iron-clad clause in his contract with the studio makes a relationship impossible. But staying away from her is out of the question.

AVAILABLE ON ALL RETAILERS.

The Lost Series

***

Lost in Us: The story of James and Serena

There are three reasons tequila is my new favorite drink.

• One: my ex-boyfriend hates it.

• Two: downing a shot looks way sexier than sipping my usual Sprite.

• Three: it might give me the courage to do something my ex-boyfriend would hate even more than tequila—getting myself a rebound

The night I swap my usual Sprite with tequila, I meet James Cohen. The encounter is breathtaking. Electrifying. And best not repeated.

James is a rich entrepreneur. He likes risks and adrenaline and is used to living the high life. He's everything I'm not.

But opposites attract. Some say opposites destroy each other. Some say opposites are perfect for each other. I don't know what will James and I do to each other, but I can't stay away from him. Even though I should.

AVAILABLE ON ALL RETAILERS.

***
Found in Us: The story of Jessica and Parker

Jessica Haydn wants to leave her past behind. Hurt by one too many heartbreaks, she vows not to fall in love again. Especially not with a man like Parker, whose electrifying pull and smile bruised her ego once before. But his sexy British accent makes her crave his touch, and his blue eyes strip Jessica of all her defenses.

Parker Blakesley has no place for love in his life. He learned the hard way not to trust. He built his business empire by avoiding distractions, and using sheer determination and control. But something about Jessica makes him question everything. Not only has she a body made for sin, but her laughter fills a void inside of him.

The desire igniting between them spirals into an unstoppable passion, and so much more. Soon, neither can fight their growing emotional connection. But can two scarred souls learn to trust again? And when a mistake threatens to tear them apart, will their love be strong enough?
AVAILABLE ON ALL RETAILERS.

***
Caught in Us: The story of Dani and Damon

Damon Cooper has all the markings of a bad boy:
• A tattoo
• A bike
• An attitude to go with point one and two

In the beginning I hated him, but now I'm falling in love with him. My parents forbid us to be together, but Damon's not one to obey rules. And since I met him, neither am I.

AVAILABLE ON ALL RETAILERS.

***

Standalone USA TODAY BESTSELLER Withering Hope

Aimee's wedding is supposed to turn out perfect. Her dress, her fiancé and the location—the idyllic holiday ranch in Brazil—are perfect.

But all Aimee's plans come crashing down when the private jet that's taking her from the U.S. to the ranch—where her fiancé awaits her—defects mid-flight and the pilot is forced to perform an emergency landing in the heart of the Amazon rainforest.

With no way to reach civilization, being rescued is Aimee and Tristan's—the pilot—only hope. A slim one that slowly withers away, desperation taking its place. Because death wanders in the jungle under many forms: starvation, diseases. Beasts.

As Aimee and Tristan fight to find ways to survive, they grow closer. Together they discover that facing old, inner agonies carved by painful pasts takes just as much courage, if not even more, than facing the rainforest.

Despite her devotion to her fiancé, Aimee can't hide her feelings for Tristan—the man for whom she's slowly becoming everything. You can hide many things in the rainforest. But not lies. Or love.

Withering Hope is the story of a man who desperately needs forgiveness and the woman who brings him hope.

It is a story in which hope births wings and blooms into a love that is as beautiful and intense as it is forbidden.
AVAILABLE ON ALL RETAILERS.

***

LAYLA HAGEN